THE CHOCOLATE MOOSE MOTIVE

This Large Print Book carries the
Seal of Approval of N.A.V.H.

A CHOCOHOLIC MYSTERY

THE CHOCOLATE MOOSE MOTIVE

JoAnna Carl

THORNDIKE PRESS
A part of Gale, Cengage Learning

GALE
CENGAGE Learning®

Detroit • New York • San Francisco • New Haven, Conn • Waterville, Maine • London

GALE
CENGAGE Learning®

Thorndike Press® Large Print Mystery
The text of this Large Print edition is unabridged.
Other aspects of the book may vary from the original edition.
Set in 16 pt. Plantin.

LIBRARY OF CONGRESS CATALOGING-IN-PUBLICATION DATA

Carl, JoAnna.
 The chocolate moose motive : a chocoholic mystery / by JoAnna Carl.
  pages ; cm. — (Thorndike Press large print mystery)
  ISBN-13: 978-1-4104-5428-7 (hardcover)
  ISBN-10: 1-4104-5428-2 (hardcover)
  1. Women detectives—Michigan—Fiction. 2. Chocolate industry—Fiction.
 3. Large type books. I. Title.
 PS3569.A51977C487 2013
 813'.54—dc23   2012041562

Published in 2013 by arrangement with NAL Signet, a member of Penguin Group (USA) Inc.

In memory of the great horned owl
who used to glide above Wolf Creek
and of the owlet in the hollow cottonwood

ACKNOWLEDGMENTS

With many thanks to Janet McGee, bird expert; to Terry Mayberry of Terry's Taxidermy; to Kade McClure, managing attorney for the Lawton office of Legal Aid Services of Oklahoma; to Joe Pazoureck, CPA; and to Tracy Paquin and Susan McDermott, wonderful neighbors and on-the-spot experts on Michigan.

ACKNOWLEDGMENTS

CHAPTER 1

It all began when I accidently ran into Sissy Smith at the South Haven supermarket — twice.

Luckily, no one was injured either time.

I had never met Sissy before that day. Our contact began as I was standing in the laundry supply aisle, trying to remember which brand of fabric softener made my husband, Joe, break out in a rash around the elastic of his boxer briefs. A threatening voice rumbled from the next aisle over and aroused me from my musings.

"Sissy," it said, "I'm going to win, so why don't you just give up? Fighting the inevitable won't get you any more money."

A feminine voice answered, "Money is the root of all evil. Let me by, please."

That exchange got my attention fast. It was much more interesting than fabric softener.

The man's voice became deeper. "I have

the resources, Sissy."

"Actually, the quote is, 'The love of money is the root of all evil.' It's First Timothy, but I forget the verse. Let me by, Ace."

"You're penniless. You don't even have a job."

"Yeah, I guess I should have picked my grandparents better so I wouldn't need a job. Let. Me. By."

"I'm not going to let my grandson be raised in a hovel."

"Sticks and stones. Let me by."

"I don't intend to break your bones, but it's not safe to oppose me, Sissy."

The guy wasn't shouting. He didn't even sound particularly angry. That made his words even more frightening.

"I'm going to get him, Sissy. And if you get hurt, I've warned you. I can crush you. And I'm willing to do it."

The woman quit making her snappy replies. She just kept requesting that the man let her by.

She didn't sound scared. In fact, she sounded slightly amused. After several more exchanges she said, "What's eating you, Ace? Have the boys in the locker room been teasing you again?"

I won't repeat what the masculine voice

replied to that, but it began with "You little — !"

Scoffing at the size of this guy's anatomy had apparently touched a nerve. The masculine voice went on and on. But all the insults and the threats were spoken in this quiet, deadly monotone.

The cold-blooded way the man was insulting and threatening the woman was impossible for me to ignore. And he obviously had boxed her in and was preventing her from moving away from him. I was beginning to be afraid things might get rough.

What should I do? I considered calling a security guard, but I wasn't sure the store had one. And I considered hauling the store manager into the situation, but I wasn't sure just what he could do. I thought about calling 9-1-1 on my cell phone, but I'd heard no threat of immediate violence.

I decided my next step was to get a look at the people in the adjacent aisle.

Moving rapidly, I shoved my cart down to the end of the fabric softener display and did a U-turn to the left, into the aisle where the ugly talking was going on.

A slender man jumped aside, and I crashed head-on into Sissy's cart. At least, I assumed it was Sissy's cart. There were only two people in the aisle.

I yanked my cart back, pretending to be contrite. "Oh! I do oppose. I mean, apologize!" Darn! My tongue has a habit of getting twisted. Once again it had embarrassed me.

"It's all right. These carts are tough, and so am I." Sissy's voice was still controlled, but it was determined. She was a tiny thing — five-one or -two, small boned, and delicate. Eyes of an unusual sea green looked at me boldly, and a sheet of glossy black hair swung out as she turned her head. I was facing a very striking young woman.

She pulled her cart back a few inches and moved it to her right. Then she went around me, ignoring the man she'd been arguing with. At the end of the aisle she turned left, walking rapidly toward the canned goods section.

I pushed my cart so that it blocked most of the aisle. I hoped this would keep the man from following her, and it worked. I was standing amidst racks of paper towels and toilet paper, alone with the man who had talked in such an ugly manner.

I turned toward him, ready to face a monster. But instead, I saw a handsome man, probably around sixty, sleek and smiling suavely. He was casually dressed — khakis, a knit shirt in a soft blue, and Top-

Siders — and his outfit was high-end. His features were regular, and he had a beautiful head of white hair. He had a cart, too. It contained several packages of meat and some prewrapped potatoes, the ready-for-the-microwave kind single men buy.

He smiled and spoke. "We need collision insurance to navigate this place, don't we?" Then he spun his cart toward the other end of the aisle and walked away, graciousness personified.

He was definitely a summer person.

I don't shop in South Haven all that often. My usual hangout is Warner Pier, twenty miles away and one-third the size of South Haven. But I'd been delivering chocolate to that particular supermarket, so I'd decided to do my shopping there as part of the trip. After all, if the South Haven supermarket was buying our chocolates, I could buy their fabric softener. Not many supermarkets carry our line of luxury European-style bonbons, truffles, and molded chocolates. They're mainly found in high-end gift and specialty shops.

I'm Lee McKinney Woodyard, and I'm business manager for TenHuis Chocolade, located in Warner Pier, Michigan. My aunt is the expert chocolatier who owns the company and supervises making the chocolates, but I'm responsible for keeping her bills paid and getting her ambrosial product to the retailers who sell it. Usually this means UPS or FedEx, but when our customer is as close to us as South Haven, I deliver.

South Haven and Warner Pier are both Lake Michigan resorts, and both draw wealthy "summer people" — such as the guy with the ugly mouth and the nice clothes — who own vacation homes in our communities. So both towns have supermarkets that aren't typical of small towns. Yes, it takes a special small-town market to stock prime beef, thirty kinds of imported cheese, and out-of-season fruits. And now the South Haven market had decided to add a selection of fancy chocolates. Naturally — ahem — they'd asked TenHuis Chocolade to supply a dozen flavors of bonbons and truffles, plus an assortment of our special molded items. This summer's special items were Michigan animals. Aunt Nettie and her genius crew were producing beautiful chocolate deer, moose, otters, raccoons, and foxes.

Our part of west Michigan has some of the most beautiful beaches in the world, and it's been a resort area for well over a hundred years. In summer, the dozens of towns along the shore of Lake Michigan are packed, and the people packed into them can be classified into three distinct categories — tourists, summer people, and locals.

Tourists come for short periods of time — a day or a week or two weeks. They rent rooms from motels or bed-and-breakfast inns. They come in tour buses or private cars. They tend to wear shorts and T-shirts that advertise other places they've visited, such as Lake Placid, the Indiana Dunes, and the St. Louis Arch. Sometimes the shirts even say PARIS or advertise a local junior college. They clog our streets, wandering up and down and buying souvenirs.

We love 'em. They bring money to town and leave it behind.

Summer people own or lease cottages and stay the whole summer. Or at least they come for weekends. They are often members of wealthy families — property on Lake Michigan doesn't come cheap — and some of them have visited this area for generations. They dress out of the L.L. Bean catalog. If their T-shirts say anything, it's HARVARD, or at least UNIVERSITY OF MICHIGAN. Of course, not all of them are wealthy, but they all pay property taxes.

We love them, too. They bring even more money than the tourists do.

Then there are us locals. We live here year-round, and most of us make a living from tourists and summer people. We mow their lawns, put up their shutters, repair their air conditioners, roof their houses. We sell them food, clothing, gasoline, wine, hedge clippers, and — in my case — fancy chocolates. We wear shorts and tees, too, but ours tend to say things such as HERITAGE BOAT RESTORATION or TENHUIS CHOCOLADE.

After the white-haired man walked off, I went back an aisle to get my fabric softener, then moved into the grocery department. I kept an eye out for Sissy. My brief look at her had titillated my curiosity. For one thing, she seemed familiar, though I couldn't figure out just why.

Sissy had been — well, "vivid" may be the best word. That glossy black hair was gorgeous, and her green eyes were riveting. She had been wearing khaki shorts, like three-quarters of the other shoppers, but her off-white tunic was trimmed in colorful embroidery I was willing to bet had been hand done. Her sandals had a handmade look.

Even her tiny stature made her stand out, but maybe that was most noticeable from the perspective of a woman like me, since I'm five foot eleven and a half. My Dutch ancestors endowed me with natural blond

16

hair, and my Texas ancestors provided the gene for tallness. I tower over most other women and a lot of men.

Sissy was stunning and unusual. I wanted to figure out where I'd seen her before, so I tried to get another look at her. But I caught only one more glimpse, and that was clear down an aisle. She was buying a big box of Cheerios, and she disappeared into another aisle while I was looking at shredded wheat.

I didn't see her again until I backed into her in the parking lot.

Great. First I whanged into her grocery cart; then I dented her car.

My excuse for the accident is modern automobile design. I have trouble seeing out the back of my van, no matter how I twist my neck. I try to park where I can exit by pulling forward, but during the summer tourist season, that's not always possible in that particular lot, even on a Monday, so I had to back out of my parking spot, and I backed into the right-front fender of a light blue Volkswagen that seemed to come from nowhere.

We didn't hit hard, luckily. We both stopped, got out of our vehicles, and went to survey the damage. I had a dented bumper, and Sissy had a ding in her fender. The blue Volkswagen was vintage — probably forty years old — but it had been in good shape before I hit it.

Sissy looked dismayed as she surveyed the damage. Our fender bender seemed to have upset her even more than the run-in with the summer guy with the foul mouth.

"I know it's best not to admit fault," I said, "but I will say I have trouble seeing what's behind this darn van. Luckily, I have really good insurance."

"I was upset," Sissy said. "I may not have looked as carefully as I should have. Do we have to call the cops?"

"I doubt the cops want to fool with a minor accident like this, especially on private property. I think we can exchange information and go."

Anyway, Sissy and I got out our information, and I found a notebook so we could write it all down. Sissy wrote my information down first, then tore out the page and handed the notebook back with her license and insurance card.

I started copying, beginning with her license.

The name at the top wasn't Sissy, which wasn't too surprising. Her legal name was Forsythia — Forsythia Smith.

It was impossible not to comment on a name that unusual. "Forsythia!" I said. "My favorite spring flower."

Belatedly I remembered who Forsythia Smith was. Darn. I'd put my foot in it.

Sissy scowled. "My mom and dad were given to flights of fancy."

"At least no one will ever forget it."

She laughed harshly. "That's true. No one will ever forget Forsythia Smith. The southwest Michigan murderess."

CHAPTER 2

That was a conversation stopper.

I don't know if I gasped or grinned. But I do know I didn't say anything aloud. I kept copying off the information on Sissy's driver's license and insurance card, gluing my eyes on the bits of paper.

When I finished writing and looked at Sissy, she had dropped her head and was staring vacantly at the parking lot's asphalt surface. She looked desperately unhappy.

She raised her head when I handed her cards back. I tried to smile. And I spoke, but why I said what I said — well, I still don't understand it.

"Hang in there," I said. "You don't snare me. I mean, you don't scare me!"

Sissy raised her head. "You're the exception," she said. Her expression didn't change.

"I'll be in touch about your fender. If you could go on and get an estimate, it might help."

She nodded, and we each went our own way.

I guided the van out of the parking lot, cursing myself because I'd twisted my tongue again. I do that when I'm nervous, but I reminded myself that Sissy couldn't know that. She'd just think I was an idiot — if she thought about it at all.

I drove across South Haven and negotiated the crazy entrance to I-196. As I headed home, I kept thinking about Sissy and her life.

A few miles up the interstate, I pulled into a rest area and parked. I sat a few minutes, still thinking. Then I took out my cell phone and called my aunt, Nettie TenHuis Jones, at the chocolate shop.

Aunt Nettie answered the telephone herself. "TenHuis Chocolade."

"Hi," I said. "How would you and Hogan like to come over for dinner tonight?"

"That sounds wonderful. We've had a really busy day here, and it would be delightful not to cook. And I sure don't want to go out to dinner. In June. In Warner Pier. Not during what I'm happy to say is a successful tourist season."

"Great! Come at six thirty. Or seven. Whenever you can make it."

As soon as I hung up, I called Joe at his boat shop. He didn't answer, so I left a message, telling him I'd invited some of his in-laws for dinner and that I'd appreciate it if he'd come home ready to fire up the charcoal cooker. I ended with, "I'll do it if you're not in the mood."

Joe is always in the mood to cook out, so I didn't anticipate a problem there.

I restarted the van and headed on toward Warner Pier. My curiosity bump was still itching, longing to know more about Forsythia Smith, but I had taken steps that would lead to scratching it.

As I drove, I shoved my curiosity into my subconscious and considered dinner. And even though I'd just left the South Haven supermarket, I hadn't planned for guests. I was going to have to stop at the Warner Pier Superette.

Warner Pier, Michigan, has twenty-five hundred year-round residents. The good thing about living in an ultrasmall town is that you know everybody. The bad thing about living in an ultrasmall town is that everybody knows you, and probably knows your business, too. Or everybody thinks they do.

My mom grew up in Warner Pier, but she moved to Dallas and wound up marrying a

22

tall Texas guy and living in his hometown, Prairie Creek. Prairie Creek is about the size of Warner Pier. When my parents were divorced, the year I was sixteen, my mom moved the two of us to Dallas and got a job in a travel agency. To get me out of the way during that difficult summer, she packed me off to Michigan to work for her brother, Phil TenHuis, and his wife, Nettie, in their chocolate shop. During those three months, Aunt Nettie was truly kind to an angry teenager she barely knew. Eleven years later, when my first husband and I split up, Aunt Nettie — who by then had been widowed — didn't ask me a single question about my divorce. She just offered me a job running the business side of her shop and factory.

Twice my life had been in crisis, and each time Aunt Nettie and the chocolate shop had been a haven to me.

Things had gone well for me since I moved to Warner Pier. I got my feet back on the ground emotionally. I fell in love again, this time with Joe Woodyard, whom I consider the best-looking and smartest and maybe the nicest guy in west Michigan.

Joe began his career as a lawyer. When he got burned out on law, he bought a boat shop. Now he works three days a week for a poverty law agency in Holland and restores antique powerboats on the other days. Joe is another Warner Pier native, and Joe's mom, it just happens, runs Warner Pier's only insurance agency.

Next, Aunt Nettie — after three years as a widow — married Warner Pier's police chief, Hogan Jones.

Meanwhile — this is a really small town — Joe's mom married again, too. She married Warner Pier's mayor, another nice guy named Mike Herrera. I won't go into Mike's son being married to my best friend; the relationships are already confusing enough. If I drew a diagram of who's married to whom, who's related to whom, and who's close friends with whom, it would look like a plate of spaghetti. Let's just leave it at this — between our relatives and our friends, Joe and I know people who know nearly everything that goes on in Warner Pier and Warner County.

When it came to Forsythia Smith, self-proclaimed murderess, I knew that Police Chief Hogan Jones — the second husband of my aunt by marriage — would have all the background on her.

Now, I want to make one thing perfectly clear. That afternoon, as I was stopping at the Warner Pier Superette for steaks and a bottle of Fenn Valley red, I had no intention

24

of getting involved in Sissy Smith's life. I just wanted to know who the guy bawling her out had been, and I wanted to know why Sissy called herself a murderess.

I'm a nosy person, and that was all I had in mind. I swear.

By six thirty, I had straightened the living room and had the steaks marinating. The table was set. The salad greens were torn up. The potatoes had been rubbed with bacon fat and were baking. The sherbet was in the freezer, and my grandmother's Depression glass serving dish held chocolates — espresso cardamom, described in our literature as "rich dark chocolate filling flavored with chocolate espresso beans and laced with a hint of cardamom, then enrobed with dark chocolate."

Joe had come home early enough to take a shower. He was firing up the charcoal cooker, and I was putting snack crackers in a bowl when Aunt Nettie and Hogan pulled into the drive. Ten minutes later we were all on the screened porch, wine or beer in hand, and Joe, Aunt Nettie, and Hogan were complaining about how busy their days had been.

I waited until I'd heard about the rush order at TenHuis Chocolade, the idiot who wanted Joe to paint his 1943 mahogany

Chris-Craft with stripes of neon green, and the city councilman who was driving Hogan crazy trying to boss day-to-day operations of the five-man police department.

Aunt Nettie looked at me and smiled her sweet smile. "Lee's keeping her mouth shut. Today was her day off. I guess she just lazed around at the beach."

"Oh, I kept busy," I said. "I went down to South Haven and delivered chocolates. I bought Joe some work shirts at that little department store, and I had lunch at the bakery across the street. Then I went back to the supermarket and did some eavesdropping. I ended up by having a fender bender with a murderess."

Everybody stared at me. I picked Hogan to stare back at, raising my eyebrows. Hogan is tall and thin, and he reminds me of Abraham Lincoln.

He frowned as he spoke. "Murderess? Who's that?"

"Forsythia Smith."

"Sissy Smith? Why do you call her a murderess? And what about this eavesdropping?"

So I told the whole story. Hogan's frown became a glare. Joe got carefully deadpan, and Aunt Nettie looked more and more worried. When I got to the end, she was the first person to speak. "My goodness, Lee! You certainly ran into an interesting situation."

"It interested me," I said. "And it raised a lot of questions. Such as, who was this Ace? Why did he tear into Sissy Smith so viciously? And why did Sissy identify herself as a murderess?"

Hogan was still frowning. "You surely remember the Buzz Smith case."

"I don't remember too much about it. Didn't it happen in February?"

"Oh yeah. I guess that was when you and Joe were in Texas for three weeks."

"Well, I did hear that Buzz Smith's wife came home and found him shot to death. But I never heard that she had been accused of killing him."

Joe spoke. "Gossip!" His voice was full of contempt. "It's given Sissy a whole bunch of trouble. She consulted our agency about this custody deal, and the whole basis of it is gossip."

Aunt Nettie nodded. "I keep hoping that story will go away."

"Nope," Hogan said. "The sheriff told me last week that he was still having citizens drop in to ask why he hasn't arrested her."

"Wait!" I said. "Will somebody explain all this? To begin with, who are Sissy and Ace?

27

I don't mean just their names. I mean, where did they come from? How long have they been here? Why don't I know them? Are they locals?"

Joe and Hogan looked at Aunt Nettie. She sighed and began. "Sissy is a local. I guess she's a sort of holdover from the hippies."

"The hippies," I said, "were fifty years ago, and Sissy can't be more than twenty-two or twenty-three."

"That's right. About forty-five years ago, Sissy's grandparents were part of a group that formed a commune about ten miles east of Warner Pier. Out in the woods."

I knew the area she meant. Warner Pier looks west over Lake Michigan. We have lots of trees, but it feels open because of the lake and because a town has streets and lawns, so it's not all trees. To our east, inland from Lake Michigan, the terrain is heavily wooded. It's flat, but there are lots of trees and bushes.

I was raised in open country, out on the plains of Texas. That area east of Warner Pier gives me the willies. The trees grow right down to the road. Plus, there's thick undergrowth. You can't see twenty feet in any direction. When I go over that way — to drive to the township dump, for example — I can hardly breathe.

Aunt Nettie said that in the sixties a group of fifteen or twenty people — Warner County had called them "the hippies" — had moved in over there on land one of them had inherited. There was one good-sized house on the property, plus a smaller house, and they all lived in those in the winter, and some of them camped outdoors in the summer.

"There was one open field on the property," she said. "They tried to grow strawberries and tomatoes. They had a little fruit stand, but it didn't work out. There wasn't work or profit enough to support that many people."

The experiment lasted only a year or two, she said; then most of the group drifted away. Only the original owner of the property, a woman who called herself Wildflower, had stayed, along with her son.

"Wildflower started a new business," Aunt Nettie said.

"Oh," I said. "I know the place you're talking about! The taxidermy shop! It has a professionally painted sign that says 'Taxidermy.' And there's a homemade sign that says 'Moose Lodge.'"

Aunt Nettie nodded. "Right. Wildflower is a taxidermist. I think the Moose Lodge sign is a joke. The place has nothing to do with the fraternal organization."

Hogan spoke. "Wildflower has a moose head over the fireplace, and the insides of the houses are rustic, like hunting lodges. I guess that's why she calls the property Moose Lodge."

"Aha," I said. "I understand that middle-aged gents don't congregate there on Saturday night to play pool — or whatever Moose members do. But I've never seen the taxidermy shop. I guess it's back from the road."

Hogan nodded. "Right. It's not visible until you're well onto the property. But Wildflower has a well-equipped shop. And by the way, she does have a last name. It's Hill."

"Wildflower Hill?" I was incredulous. "You've gotta be kidding."

"I've seen her driver's license," Hogan said.

Aunt Nettie went on. "Wildflower is considered something of a recluse. Her son — I don't remember what his name was — worked as a carpenter. He married a Hispanic girl named Maria. But the son was killed in a car wreck, and Maria died of cancer when Sissy, their daughter, was ten or eleven. Sissy has always lived there with her grandmother."

"It sounds as if Sissy's had a hard life.

Her parents died young, and her only relative was a grandmother who was probably considered odd by the neighbors."

"That's true, but it didn't seem to hold Sissy back," Aunt Nettie said. "She went to Warner Pier High, and I remember seeing her picture in the paper when she made the honor society. She worked as a waitress, saved her money, and was able to go to the junior college for a year or so. She probably got a scholarship. But then she made a big mistake."

"What was that?"

"She dated a boy from a summer family."

I laughed. "Oh no! Not a dreaded summer guy?"

When I came to Warner Pier at age sixteen to work in the small retail shop at TenHuis Chocolade, the first thing the other counter girls told me was, "Never date a summer guy." It would, they said, ruin your reputation with the Warner Pier high school crowd.

Of course, some of the summer people were extremely wealthy, which might tend to make them attractive to some girls, but I could readily see the problems "summer guys" might produce. First, their wealthy families might object to the local girls, who were likely to come from undistinguished families. Second, the summer guys were go-

31

ing to go home at the end of August, and if the local boys were snubbing you, the winter might get lonely.

So Warner Pier was friendly to the summer people, but it was considered unwise for local girls to date them.

I'd always thought the whole thing was silly, so I laughed. But Joe, Aunt Nettie, and Hogan didn't.

"Who did Sissy date?" I said.

"Rupert Smith the Fourth," Hogan said. "Nicknamed Buzz."

"The guy who was killed."

"Right. He married Sissy, even though his family supposedly wasn't very happy about it."

"And who is his family? I never heard of a Rupert Smith the Third."

"Not even the Smiths go by their numbers. They all have crazy nicknames. His dad is known as Ace Smith. There's a cousin called Spud, and another cousin who goes by Deuce. I think there's a Chip, as well. Most of them live in Chicago. Or else they're in the army somewhere. The family tends toward the military. Ace is a retired colonel."

"Ace is Buzz's dad? So he was the one who was lambasting Sissy at the supermarket?"

32

Hogan grimaced. "Sissy and Buzz had a little boy. He must be over a year old now. I'd heard that Ace was trying to get custody of the kid, trying to prove Sissy is an unfit mother."

"Has the welfare department looked into it?"

"Yes, and they didn't find anything wrong. So Ace has hired private eyes."

"Oh, Lordy! Now I'm on Sissy's side!"

All the people present knew that my first husband had sicced private eyes on me during our divorce. It wasn't a pleasant experience, even though they didn't find any evidence that helped him.

"I think Sissy came to be sorry she took up with Buzz," Hogan said. "Ace wouldn't help them, and Buzz couldn't hold a job. Sissy might have thought she was marrying money, but she had to support the family. I doubt Wildflower makes very much from her taxidermy business, so Sissy probably helped her, too. Sissy worked in Holland, keeping books for one of the office furniture companies."

"Why did Ace lambast her for not even having a job?"

"I don't know. She must have been laid off. But at the time Buzz was killed, Sissy was working. As near as I could find out,

Buzz didn't do anything around there to help out. Sissy and her grandmother were on a shopping trip to Holland when Buzz was killed. And they had taken the little boy with them. Sissy took him to day care during the week. Apparently Buzz didn't even babysit."

Buzz had been killed on a Saturday, Hogan said. Sissy and Wildflower had left at midmorning. They were driving two cars, Sissy's antique blue Volkswagen and a VW van of similar vintage, which Wildflower drove. They dropped Sissy's car at a Holland garage, arranging to pick it up on Tuesday. Then they had lunch at Russ', a Holland restaurant. They'd made the regular Holland round — JCPenney for pajamas for the little boy, the health food store for some things Wildflower ate, Office Depot for ink for Sissy's computer printer, and two carts of groceries at Family Fare.

"That's why we know for sure Sissy wasn't home shooting her husband," Hogan said. "She's striking — with that black hair and those green eyes — and Wildflower is unconventional looking, too. Plus, they're regulars at the health food store, so the people there remembered them. Their waitress at Russ' remembered them. The only place they went that nobody remembered them was the gas station. And they had a credit card slip from there."

When they returned home, to the old house where the hippies had once lived, the little boy was asleep in his car seat. Sissy began to lift him out, and Wildflower took a bag of groceries inside. She found Buzz dead in the living room.

Wildflower called to Sissy, telling her not to bring the little boy in. Sissy ran inside, leaving her sleeping son in the car. Buzz had been dead long enough that his body was beginning to cool. They called 9-1-1 on Sissy's cell phone. Wildflower waited for the sheriff in Sissy's car, but Sissy had stayed inside with Buzz's body.

"It didn't seem right to leave him alone," she had told Hogan later.

Buzz had died from a single gunshot wound in the head. Suicide was ruled out, Hogan said. The position of the wound was wrong, and the gun was missing.

The medical examiner later put the time of death at around noon, and the ballistics experts said the murder weapon was a .45 caliber pistol.

"So," Hogan said, "Sissy and Wildflower both have good alibis."

"Could Buzz have been shot before they left for Holland?"

"The ME didn't think so."

"Then how could this rumor that Sissy killed her husband get started?"

Hogan's glare came back. "The problem is, Sissy is her own worst enemy."

CHAPTER 3

Naturally we all wanted to know why Sissy was her own worst enemy. Two *why*s and a *how* rang out.

Hogan stared at the porch floor and took a swig of his beer before he spoke. Even then he didn't answer our questions. "This wasn't my case," he said.

"You mean Buzz Smith's death?" I said. "We know that, Hogan. Buzz died in a rural area east of Warner Pier. This Moose Lodge where Sissy's grandmother lives is at least fifteen miles outside our city limits, so it would have been a case for Sheriff Ramsey. Plus, the way rural crime is investigated in Michigan means that the state police would come in anyway. Right?"

"Right. But Warner County doesn't have loads of law-enforcement officers. So last February, when I heard there was a killing, I went out there, just to see if Burt Ramsey needed help. Burt gave me the job of staying with Sissy and her grandmother."

"So you were the first law-enforcement official to have contact with her."

"One of the first."

"And you thought Sissy was her own worst enemy. Why?"

Hogan sighed. "Sissy has a smart mouth."

"You mean she makes wisecracks?"

Hogan nodded.

"That's not usually a crime."

"Sissy seems to have a talent for making wisecracks at exactly the wrong moment. The day Buzz was killed, for example, when the EMTs arrived, she said, 'At least you won't have to hunt around for the wound.' "

Joe and Aunt Nettie looked puzzled, and I'm sure I did, too.

Hogan explained. "Buzz had his head shaved. He was shot in the back of the head. He didn't even have any hair to hide the wound." His voice trailed off.

"That wasn't so bad, Hogan," I said.

"Maybe the words weren't so bad. I guess it was her sarcastic tone."

"Maybe she was just nervous. If she'd been sitting with his body . . . that would have shattered anybody's nerves. Was she crying?"

"No." Hogan's voice was sharp. "And I don't hold that against her. I've seen people hit by bad news hundreds of times. They all react differently. Some of them cry. Some get hysterical. Some are sort of frozen. But it's unusual for people to start making funny remarks."

"She kept making wisecracks?"

"When the neighbors showed up, Sissy said to her grandmother, 'Nosy and Rosy are here.' And her grandmother shushed her, but Sissy went on. She said, 'I guess they don't want to miss anything.' "

"That may not have been tactful, but it's understandable. I've sure known people who show up during a crisis out of curiosity, not kindness. If these people were neighbors, I guess Sissy knew them. Nosy and Rosy were probably nicknames they used all the time."

"What Sissy said about the neighbors was nothing to what she said about the TV reporters when they showed up."

"I can't blame her for that." I'd had my own run-ins with television reporters.

Hogan laughed. "It was that jerk Gordon Hitchcock. She called him 'the ghoul.' I pretty much agreed with her. Unfortunately, he heard her, and that didn't encourage the station to give her a break on the air. Then I heard that the next day, when some of the neighbors brought food, she wasn't tactful about it. 'We don't need charity.' That sort of remark."

"That was too bad. But it sounds as if the grandmother is the one considered odd by the neighbors. How did she react?"

"Oh, I'd say she was pretty normal, at least while I was here. Normal for her. She mainly kept an eye on the baby. She took him into Sissy's house." He looked up. "And by the way, the houses out there may look like shacks from the outside, but there's nothing wrong with them inside. The houses aren't — well, like what you'd see in a magazine, but they're comfortable. The plumbing works. The electricity is on. Both houses are pretty rustic, but I think that's because Wildflower and Sissy like to live that way."

"Did the sheriff ask them to leave the property for the investigation?"

"Just until the next day. The neighbors — Nosy and Rosy — offered to take them in, but Sissy said she'd rather go to a hotel, even if it meant going to South Haven or Holland. She wasn't very gracious about it. Actually, Sarajane found rooms for them."

Sarajane Harding is a close friend of Aunt Nettie's. She runs a bed-and-breakfast inn.

"I hope the sheriff paid for it," I said. "Sarajane's rates are steep, even in the winter, and I'm sure Sissy and her grandmother don't have a lot of money."

"Burt and Sarajane worked it out, but Sissy and Wildflower kept insisting they could pay their own way." He went on, frowning. "Paying their own way seems to be a thing with both of them. They don't like for anybody to act as though they're poor."

"Even though they are poor?"

"I guess that's when it's hardest to take," Hogan said. "Keeping up appearances. You know."

"Like the March girls each clutching one glove at the ball," I said.

Hogan looked confused. I didn't try to explain. I guess boys don't read Louisa May Alcott, so men don't remember how hard *Little Women*'s Jo, Meg, Beth, and Amy worked to face respectable New England society in the 1860s. Their efforts to get matching pairs of kid gloves together for a ball made a big impression on a little girl in Texas who didn't have many good clothes herself. Looking back, even in high school I can remember assuring everyone I thought the new fashions were ugly, whereas the truth was that my babysitting money wouldn't stretch far enough to buy the latest thing, and I knew my mother couldn't afford to buy me clothes.

Suddenly I felt a real kinship with Sissy Smith. I blinked, hard. "And now she's apparently lost her job," I said.

Aunt Nettie smiled. She has a truly sweet smile, and it accurately reflects her disposition. "I guess we could give her one," she said. "I can always use more hands in the workroom."

I looked at Hogan and raised my eyebrows. "What would you think of that?"

"I wouldn't know of any reason not to hire her," he said. "But I'm not sure she'd be good at making chocolate. She's a bookkeeper, you know."

"Even better!" Aunt Nettie's voice was happy. "I've been trying to get you to hire an assistant, Lee."

This was true. Several times Aunt Nettie had suggested I needed help with the business side. Now she was pushing the idea again.

I tried to react cautiously. "I'll have to see Sissy about this accident. Maybe I can talk to her informally."

Joe jumped into the conversation then. "Sissy came to our agency over the custody case," he said. "I think she tries to put up a tough facade to hide her insecurities. But you could offer her a job for the summer, and if she drives you crazy, you could let her go next fall."

Then he turned to Hogan with a question about Warner Pier crime rates. This effectively changed the subject, and it was time, I think. We were all about to get weepy over Sissy Smith.

I tried to remind myself that I didn't really know her. I'd heard her father-in-law talking ugly to her, and we'd exchanged information after our fender bender. I had felt sorry for her, and Hogan's tale had made me feel even more sorry for her.

Feeling sorry for someone wasn't a good basis for hiring the individual. I knew I probably ought to forget the whole thing.

But I didn't do that. After Aunt Nettie and Hogan left that evening, I got on the computer, searched for west Michigan job-hunting sites, and found Sissy's résumé posted.

Hmmm. She'd completed a course in the bookkeeping program TenHuis Chocolade used.

But we're a small business. All our employees have to be ready to work at the retail counter. They have to be able to meet the public. A wisecracker might not be real good at that.

In a small business all the employees have

to get along, too. If the hairnet ladies — the geniuses who actually make our delectable bonbons and truffles — thought Sissy Smith was a murderess . . . Well, it might be unjust, but if they all thought that, hiring Sissy might simply cause her more trouble. Working in an unfriendly environment could make things worse. I went to bed worried.

But I did call her previous employer — listed in the online résumé — and he gave her a glowing recommendation. She had resigned because the turmoil that followed Buzz's death had made it too difficult for her to work, he said.

Two days later, when Sissy called to tell me how much it would cost to repair her car, and it was only a couple of hundred dollars, I told her I'd just write her a check and forget the insurance claim. I added, "I ran across your résumé on line. We're looking for a bookkeeper. Would you be interested in talking to me about the job?"

Then I gritted my teeth and hoped she'd say no. I still felt nervous about the whole deal. Did we really want to hire a woman from an odd family who had been the subject of a lot of gossip? Would I have the nerve to tell Sissy Smith that she'd have to restrain that glossy black hair if she wanted to work in a food establishment?

But after a pause Sissy said she was interested. When she came by that afternoon, her hair was in a bun, and she was wearing a businesslike dark dress. She brought her résumé along in a manila folder.

Her attitude was admittedly wary. "I guess you know my husband was a murder victim," she said.

I tried to make my attitude completely clear. "I guess you know my aunt is married to Chief Hogan Jones," I said. "And, yes, sometimes we talk about local crime."

"So you've heard the gossip about me." She stared at me with those bold green eyes.

I stared back, still determined to be upfront with her. "If you were around town last winter, I guess you heard I was a suspect in a murder case. But I didn't do it."

Sissy smiled a wry smile. "I didn't either."

"Okay," I said. "So we agree not to listen to gossip."

She nodded. "Deal. Now, what accounting program are you using?"

The rest of the interview was standard. I had her résumé, so we just skimmed over her past job experience. Sissy said she had liked her previous job.

"Things were so hectic for me after Buzz

was killed that I finally had to quit," she said, "but we parted on good terms."

She asked about our yearly budget, and I told her that I particularly wanted someone to take care of payroll.

She nodded confidently. "I've done that. How many employees do you have?"

I showed her the crummy little room we'd planned to fix up for her to work in, then gave her a quick tour of the rest of the place. I made sure she understood this was just a summer job. I was afraid to plan farther ahead than that.

The only touchy moment came when I introduced her to Aunt Nettie's chief chocolate-making assistant, Dolly Jolly, who is quite striking. She's tall and broad and has red hair that almost glows.

As I said, I'm five feet eleven and a bit, but Dolly towers over me. At just over five feet, Sissy looked like a doll next to the two of us. She stepped back and looked up as if we were two skyscrapers. She didn't say anything, but her stance was hilarious. Dolly and I both broke into laughter.

"Don't worry, Sissy!" Dolly shouted. Dolly's voice always comes out as a shout. "We don't have a height requirement."

"We'll put your desk on stilts," I said.

For the first time, Sissy gave a broad

smile. "You two can take a joke," she said.

"Yeah, Dolly and I can," I said, "but not all our customers have well-developed senses of humor."

"I'll remember."

Dolly showed her how our molded chocolates are made, and Sissy oohed and ahhed over the clever little molded animals we were featuring that summer. The moose, of course, drew most of her compliments.

Finally, Aunt Nettie, who does own the business, after all, sat down and talked to Sissy. She finished up by asking Sissy if she had any questions.

"Just one." Sissy sighed. "My grandmother does our cooking, and she's heavily into natural food. Will you still consider me if I tell you we don't keep refined sugar in the house?"

Aunt Nettie smiled broadly. "If you have no moral objection to eating it," she said, "we'll teach you."

So we hired her. Sissy agreed to start the next Monday. We shook hands all around, and Aunt Nettie gave her a small box of chocolates — including two moose — to take with her. "To practice eating refined sugar," she said.

As she left, I felt good about the whole thing. We needed a good bookkeeper, and

47

Sissy had the skills. Sissy needed a job, and we'd been able to give her one.

Then Tracy Henderson, one of our counter girls, came into my office and shut the door behind her.

"What's up, Tracy?"

"Lee! You're not really going to hire a woman who murdered her husband, are you?"

CHAPTER 4

I looked at Tracy for a moment, then leaned forward to rest my head on my desktop. I banged my forehead against the blotter three times.

"Lee! Lee! I was only kidding!" Tracy's voice was anguished. "You've nagged me about gossiping so long that I finally got the idea."

"Aunt Nettie and I want to help Sissy out, not cause more trouble for her, Tracy. If you and the ladies who work here are going to start talking irresponsibly . . ."

Tracy was shaking her head. "No, Lee. I went to high school with Sissy. She was two years ahead of me. I've thought all along that all this talk about her was ridiculous. She's definitely not the kind of person to kill anybody. I'm on Sissy's side. I promise."

"I'm glad to hear it. But, Tracy, the best thing you can do is just shut up."

"But I'm ready to tell everyone she's innocent."

I shook my head. "I think it's better if you simply don't bring it up. The less talk the better. In this case, actions will probably speak louder than words. If you're friendly to Sissy, if you tell her it's good to be working with her and maybe go to lunch with her — then people will see you believe in her. You don't need to be protecting her all the time."

Tracy agreed to follow this policy, but I took her agreement with a grain of salt. Tracy is a talker. It's incredibly hard for her to stay quiet.

She'd barely gone back to her place behind the retail counter when Aunt Nettie came in and perched on the edge of my visitor's chair.

She looked a bit concerned. "Do you think we're doing the right thing, Lee?"

"Yes, I feel confident about that. What I'm not sure of is how well it's going to work out. Tracy's already been in. I was a bit surprised to learn she's on Sissy's side, and she's ready to tell the world Sissy wouldn't kill anybody. It seems she knew her in high school."

"I'm glad she feels that way, but it may not help."

"I agree. I tried to convince her that less

talk was a good thing. But you know Tracy. It's hard for her to shut up."

At this moment, Connie Van Doren, one of the ladies from the workshop — the people who actually make our chocolates — came to the door of the office. Connie, a stout, middle-aged lady with gray hair and delft blue eyes, stood there, frowning.

Aunt Nettie spoke. "Yes, Connie?"

"Nettie, you and Lee aren't really going to hire that awful Sissy Smith, are you?"

"Do you know some reason we shouldn't?"

"Well." Connie frowned harder. "Everyone knows she killed her husband."

Before I could lace into her, Aunt Nettie spoke. "Oh! If that's true, you'd better tell the sheriff."

"Wha-what?"

"Yes, Sheriff Ramsey has been very upset because that case is on his unsolved list. Or that was what Hogan told me. If you have new evidence, the sheriff will want to hear it."

"I don't have any evidence!"

"Then what makes you think she killed her husband?"

Connie frowned. "Well, my cousin Jenny talked to a lady who saw her car go back out to that weird, hippie place where they

51

lived — right at the time when Buzz Smith was killed."

"How did Jenny know when he was killed?"

"Well, everyone knows . . ." Connie paused. "It wasn't Jenny who knew. It was this lady she knows. And Jenny didn't tell me who it was."

"So it was the lady Jenny knows who saw the car."

"I'm not sure she *saw* the car. Maybe she knows somebody who saw it."

"Why don't you talk to Jenny and see if you can track down this unknown woman who claims she saw the car. Because I'm sure either the sheriff or the state police would be glad to hear about that. Or, once you get the facts, you could talk to Hogan. He's not directly concerned with the investigation into the death of Buzz Smith, but he's discussed the case with the sheriff, and I'm sure he'd help you get the new evidence to the right person."

Connie had the sense to look a little embarrassed. "I guess Chief Jones knows you've hired Sissy Smith."

Aunt Nettie nodded and smiled her sweetest smile. "He knows we were thinking about it. He said she ought to be a good employee."

"Oh." Connie swallowed. "Well, I'll get back to work." She left.

Aunt Nettie and I looked at each other. Neither of us spoke for a full minute. Then Aunt Nettie stood up. "I guess I'd better get back to work, too. As for Sissy, well . . . we may be in for an interesting time."

"I hope Sissy has a smart-aleck remark to handle this situation."

I went back to work, too, but if I'd been nervous about Sissy before, now I was ready to pull my hair, chew my nails, and fidget all over. I still believed Aunt Nettie and I were right to give Sissy a chance, but I dreaded Monday, Sissy's first day on the job.

But when Monday came, Sissy took her place at TenHuis Chocolade with no commotion. The hairnet ladies buzzed, of course, but they kept working, and Sissy didn't even complain about the lousy office we gave her.

TenHuis was originally set up — thirty-five years ago — as a two-person business. Aunt Nettie and Uncle Phil had spent a year in the Netherlands, doing an apprenticeship to learn the chocolate business. They returned to their hometown, Warner Pier, and opened a small shop. At first, both made chocolate and both waited on any customers who came in. Uncle Phil made a few sales calls on restaurants and specialty shops, but the business grew simply because they made wonderful bonbons and truffles and Warner Pier residents and visitors began to buy them. Then specialty shops and restaurants began to buy them. Out-of-town people began to call, write, and e-mail to order them. Now we sell more chocolate out of town than we do in Warner Pier. We're well acquainted with the FedEx and UPS drivers.

After they'd been in business a year or so, Aunt Nettie and Uncle Phil needed to hire more help, and eventually the business operation shook out with Aunt Nettie managing the workshop and overseeing the twenty-five or so ladies who make the chocolates, and Uncle Phil handling the business and shipping ends and supervising the small retail shop.

After Uncle Phil died, Aunt Nettie hired me to run the business side. But through all this, the shop had remained at the same address. Things changed, of course. The building they were in went on the market, so they bought it. The store next door closed, so they expanded into that space. As the mail-order business grew, they added a shipping room at the back. But the workshop and retail store remained small, and my office was an eight-by-eight glass cubicle overlooking the retail area on one side and the workshop on another.

Until Sissy started work, that office housed the whole business department. I definitely couldn't share it with another person; it would barely hold my desk. So we had adapted a small storage room for Sissy. She and I had to walk through a corner of the shop to reach each other, though we did have an intercom as part of our telephone system. But Sissy was pretty much stuck in a closet — a well-ventilated closet, but a very small space in an inconspicuous part of the business.

Until the parade started, I hadn't realized this would turn out to be a big advantage. Because beginning Monday morning, we had a small boom in business.

The retail shop is always busy during the summer tourist season, but that morning we weren't drawing tourists. No, we were invaded by locals.

Barbara, manager of our bank branch, came in to buy a half pound of Amaretto truffles ("milk chocolate filling flavored with almond liqueur, enrobed in milk chocolate, and dusted with chopped almonds").

"These are my mom's favorites," she said,

"and tomorrow is her birthday."

She spoke a little too casually, and she looked all around the office and the shop. It was obvious Barbara was checking out the news that we'd hired Sissy Smith.

"Nice present," I said. "I'm glad you came in. I want you to meet our new bookkeeper. She'll be doing some of our banking."

"Oh! You've finally hired some office help?"

"Sure have."

We both sounded as innocent as lambs.

I took Barbara's money, then led her back to Sissy's little office. The two of them shook hands, and we all acted friendly and casual.

It was after Barbara left that Sissy spoke. "The gauntlet begins," she said. "Everybody's going to want to get a look at me."

"Warner Pier is a small town," I said. "There aren't that many people to come by for a look. How are you coming with the payroll records?"

"You haven't asked me to do anything complicated yet."

"I warned you the job would be routine."

"Routine sounds great. After the past four months, I love routine."

Barbara's visit set the pattern for the day.

At ten thirty, Sarajane, the B and B owner,

came in personally to buy five pounds of mint truffles ("dark chocolate mint-flavored filling, covered in dark chocolate, and embellished with pale green stripes"). She buys these all the time to place on her guests' pillows, but usually she expects me to deliver them.

At eleven o'clock, Jason Foster, who runs the Warner Point Restaurant, bought several pounds of Kahlúa truffles ("milk chocolate centers, flavored with coffee liqueur, covered with milk chocolate and decorated with dark chocolate stripes"). He said he was going to experiment with offering them to accompany after-dinner coffee. Since Jason already offers a fabulous dessert cart, I didn't really expect him to add TenHuis chocolates to his menu, but I didn't turn down the money.

After lunch, four Warner Pier teachers came in and indulged in just one bonbon each. One had Asian spice ("milk chocolate center flavored with exotic spices and enrobed in milk chocolate, then embellished with ground ginger"). Two had French vanilla ("milk chocolate center with a milk chocolate coating, decorated with crumbled white chocolate"). The fourth went for nocturne, our darkest chocolate. Both center and coating are dark chocolate, and it's even decorated with shaved dark chocolate. I could hear them telling the counter girls that they'd skipped the fabulous peach melba at Herrera's, the town's most elegant restaurant, so they could each splurge on a TenHuis chocolate.

None of these people got a look at Sissy, however. She was occupied in her office, and I didn't offer to call her out to put her on display.

About fifteen or twenty other Warner Pier people came in — people I wouldn't have expected to see, that is. In June, most of our customers are tourists, with a sprinkling of summer people. But that day it seemed that lots of locals had decided they needed expensive chocolate.

In fact, I began to get a bit annoyed at the parade. It was so obvious that they wanted to gawk at Sissy. Then I reminded myself to have a sense of humor. The "new" would wear off soon enough. People would get used to Sissy as a regular part of our downtown scene.

Or that was what I thought until about four forty-five.

That was when Sissy came around to my office, and at the same time a woman I didn't know walked in the front door.

I immediately knew something was wrong.

Sissy took a deep breath, and the tension in the shop grew as thick as my grandma's mashed-potato soup.

The woman was slightly familiar, in the way that nearly everybody in a town this small is familiar. I'd probably seen her at the grocery store or the post office. But I didn't know her.

I guessed her age at mid-fifties. Her most distinctive feature was that she layered her makeup on with a trowel, and her second most distinctive feature was phony blond hair.

Okay, I admit that as a natural blonde, I'm critical of other people's dye jobs. I have a rather smug feeling that they're going to work hard and spend a lot of money, but the light blond hair I got from my Dutch ancestors is still going to look better than their expensive dos. But this hair was really awful. The color was harsh and the texture dry. Why anyone would want to have hair like that was beyond me.

The other thing I didn't understand was the stillness that fell over Sissy and the woman.

Then Sissy spoke, and the stillness went away. "Hello, Helen," she said. "Still busy spreading joy everywhere?"

CHOCOLATE CHAT

Since its earliest days, chocolate has been assigned medicinal or health functions.

Chocolate was cultivated by the Olmec Indians in South America as early as 1500 BC. By the time Europeans entered the picture in the 1500s, it was grown, processed, and used by many tribes in South and Central America and by the Aztecs in Mexico. At that time, chocolate was a bitter drink, and it was too expensive for ordinary people. Only the wealthiest and most important could afford it.

Those ancient chocoholics believed chocolate brought wisdom, knowledge, vitality, strength, and other qualities associated with good health.

The Aztec emperor Montezuma reportedly drank chocolate before visiting his harem. Was this the first link of chocolate with romance?

Over the years, chocolate was credited with relieving diarrhea and even improving an upset stomach caused by a hangover. Chocolate makers said their product encouraged sleep, cured the common cold, brought quick energy, and eased mental stress. Plus, they claimed it even reduced belching.

CHAPTER 5

"I try, Sissy!" The woman's voice dripped sugar sweeter than anything TenHuis Chocolade sells. She hadn't seemed to notice the sarcastic edge to Sissy's voice. "You're looking as pretty as ever!"

"Thanks, Helen."

Sissy turned toward me, but the new customer kept talking. "And how's that darling little boy of yours?"

"He's fine."

"His grandpa would sure love to see him."

Sissy's only answer was a smile — a rather strained smile. Then she turned away from the woman and spoke to me. "I have a question, Lee."

"Sure," I said.

Sissy closed the door and stepped closer to my desk. Since the door to my office is just a sheet of glass, that didn't accomplish much, but at least it gave the illusion of privacy.

"If you're going to tell secrets," I said, speaking in a low voice, "I'd better warn you this office is not soundproof."

"No secrets. I just had a question about Tracy's hours."

She handed me Tracy's time sheet, and we both looked at it, with our heads close together.

I spoke in a whisper. "Who's the old bag with the slut makeup?"

Sissy broke up. Rarely have I had such a reaction to a remark, at least one I have made to be deliberately funny. Because of my habit — maybe I'd better call it an affliction — of getting my tongue tangled, I frequently get unsought laughs, but I'm not exactly witty.

My little funny broke the tension, and Sissy whooped with laughter. "I'll tell you later," she said.

We settled Tracy's time card quickly, and Sissy left. She nodded to Helen and walked rapidly toward her cubbyhole. But the woman with the homemade blond hair called out before Sissy escaped.

"Oh, Sissy! How is your grandmother?"

Sissy slowed, but she kept walking. "Fine," she said. Then she disappeared into the back.

"Helen," whoever she was, stuck around

until nearly five o'clock, asking the counter girls questions about every item in the showcase. She finally selected a four-piece box of blackberry truffles ("dark chocolate filling flavored with real Michigan blackberries, covered with dark chocolate and embellished with a swirl of purple").

As soon as she was out the door, I headed back to Sissy's office and sat down in the one extra chair. "Now, who the heck is Helen?"

Sissy hesitated, so I spoke again. "I'm sure you've already discovered that I'm a deeply nosy person. If it's none of my business, just tell me to get lost."

"Oh, there's no secret. Helen Ferguson works for Ace Smith, my father-in-law. She calls herself his housekeeper. Which is a fancy term for cleaning woman."

"Housekeeper sounds as if she heads a staff."

"Unless things have changed for Ace, he doesn't have a staff. Buzz's mom died twelve years ago, and Ace batches it. The few times I was at his house, the house looked as if some old bachelor lived there. I think Helen comes once a week and shovels it out."

Sissy clenched her hands together and stared at her interlocked fingers. "Helen and

I never liked each other. I'm sure that was obvious."

"How come she dyes her hair that odd color?"

"I'm afraid that was my fault. After Ace became a full-time resident of Warner Pier three years ago, Helen began to play up to him. It became a sort of joke to Buzz and me, but Ace seemed oblivious to what was going on.

"I began to feel sorry for her. I decided she needed to be discouraged in her pursuit. Finally, I made a remark something like, 'If Ace fell for anyone, it would probably be some ditsy blonde.' The next time I saw Helen . . ." She shook her head.

"She'd become a ditsy blonde."

"Right." Sissy looked up. "I guess I feel guilty about it. I'm sure Ace has no interest in Helen. He treats her like part of the furniture. Then there was another complication — Helen's daughter, Fran. Helen used to push her at Buzz."

"So both Helen and Fran may have seen you as a rival of sorts."

"Actually, I don't think Fran ever had any interest in Buzz. Buzz certainly never had any interest in her. But Helen is one of these women who think it's good to be chased by lots of men. She was always telling people

64

how popular her daughter was and pushed her to wear sexy clothes and act in ways — well, ways my grandmother didn't encourage. In high school, Fran's popularity wasn't always the kind everyone envies."

"The class slut?"

"I wouldn't go that far. More the class tease. Fran is married now, and I think she lives in Grand Rapids."

Sissy and I both sighed. I couldn't think of any remark to make about the situation with Helen, so I changed the subject. "Any comments after your first day at TenHuis?"

"I'm glad you put a limit on how much chocolate the employees can eat. I could gain a lot of weight."

"Two pieces a day. And I eat both of mine every day. Is your grandmother shocked at your working for people whose livelihood is based on refined sugar?"

"Not at all. She thinks each of us should follow his own conscience. Her diet ideas are preferences, not moral choices."

"I'd like to meet her."

Sissy laughed. "She's a character!"

We discussed a few more things, and it was time to close up. The workroom and the business office close at five. The retail shop stays open until nine during the tourist season.

I went back to my office to get my purse. I felt that Sissy had made a good start on her job, and the ladies in the shop had seemed to accept her without drama.

Which showed what I knew, because at that moment the next act of the play began.

Enter: a good-looking guy with a lot of star power.

He didn't leap in like a swashbuckler or fall in like a comedian. He simply opened the street door and walked in. But he gave the effect of being announced by a fanfare of trumpets and illuminated by a spotlight.

The newcomer had handsome features, true, but it wasn't just his looks that brought attention. Personality oozed from every pore. He was tall, with sandy blond hair, broad shoulders, and a grin that was just slightly crooked.

Behind the counter, Tracy caught her breath, and the second counter girl, Mary Ann, dropped a bonbon on the floor. My jaw began to fall; I barely caught it before it hit the desk. Time seemed to stand still. All three of us simply stared at him.

The guy walked over to the counter, grinned his crooked grin, and spoke. "Is Sissy Smith still here?"

Time began moving again when we heard his voice. Not that there was anything wrong with his voice, which was a pleasant baritone. But he didn't issue a call to arms or break into song. He simply spoke in an ordinary tone.

Tracy answered in a breathy whisper. "Sissy's in the back."

The newcomer was still smiling. "I wanted to give her these," he said. And he held up a bouquet. I'd been so fascinated by the guy that I hadn't noticed he was carrying it.

The bouquet was centered with tiny white flowers, almost like wildflowers. These were surrounded by broad green leaves. It was very different from the usual florist's offering.

Tracy moved to the door to the shop and called out. "Sissy!" This time her voice squeaked.

Sissy walked around the corner with her head down. She was digging in her purse and held two TenHuis T-shirts (optional wear for business office employees) under her arm. "I'm coming," she said. "Or, rather, I'm going. I've got to pick up the kid. Did I forget something?"

Tracy squeaked again. "Someone's here to see you."

Sissy looked up then. Her face was as blank as everyone else's face for a moment. Then she spoke. "Chip!"

She had stopped in the doorway to the shop, but the handsome guy moved around the end of the counter to meet her.

"It's sure good to see you," he said, then leaned way over and tried to kiss her. I think he aimed for her mouth, but Sissy stepped backward, and he missed. All she got was an air kiss.

"What in the world are you doing here?"

"I brought you flowers."

"Oh. Well, thanks. But what are you doing in Warner Pier?"

"I have a month's leave."

"Are you staying with Ace?"

"Yes."

"Better not let him find out you came to see me, or you'll be going to a hotel."

"I told him I was going to see you, and he didn't warn me off. How about a quick drink?"

Sissy shook her head. "No thanks, Chip. I have to pick up Johnny."

"Later? Tomorrow?"

"Thanks, but I don't think that's a good idea."

I suddenly realized I was staring, watching the whole scene as if it were any of my business. Wake up, I told myself firmly. Mind your own business for once.

I slammed my desk drawer and moved

toward my office door. Of course, to get to my parking space behind the shop I had to pass Sissy and the big handsome guy. I turned sideways and tried to edge past them.

"Lee." Sissy stopped me. "This is Chip Smith. He's Buzz's cousin, and he was also his best friend."

We shook hands and made polite noises.

"I overheard you say you're on leave, Chip," I said. "Are you serving in the military?"

"No, I work for a defense contractor. I've been posted abroad for two years."

"That sounds like hard duty."

"Not so bad."

All this time we'd had the door between the shop and the workroom blocked, and I became aware that Sissy was trying to edge toward the front of the shop. I moved aside, trying to open a path for her. "Did you say you need to pick up your little boy, Sissy?"

"Yes, I do. Chip, it's great to see you."

"I want to see Johnny, too. He was brand-new the last time I was home."

"That would be nice. Call me and we'll arrange a playdate for you. But be sure you feel up to a strenuous piggyback session."

She and Chip both laughed, and he also turned toward the outside door. "At least I can walk you to your car."

All of us in the shop — Tracy, Mary Ann, and I — were concentrating on Sissy and Chip, and Sissy and Chip were concentrating on each other. I guess that was why the loud banging noise made all five of us jump about a foot off the floor.

We all whirled toward the sound, each of us gasping or even, in Tracy's case, giving a tiny scream.

The noise, I realized, had merely been someone rapping on the window.

And that someone was Ace Smith, Sissy's father-in-law.

He was standing outside, peering inside, a hand raised as a shield against the sun.

Sissy stopped short. "Chip, you go on without me," she said.

"Sissy . . ."

"I don't want to see Ace today. I'm sure you understand."

Chip's big friendly face took on a miserable expression, but he nodded and left without further questions.

"Come on, Sissy," I said. "We'll go out the back, and I'll give you a ride over to the parking lot."

"Thanks, Lee. I didn't mean to insert my family problems into the workplace. I'll try not to do it again."

So Sissy and I talked about other things as I drove the two blocks to Warner Pier's downtown parking lot, where one section is reserved for local employees. I resisted asking her about Chip, and she told me about Johnny, who was fourteen months old. He was, she reported proudly, a beautiful, intelligent, and lively little boy. We parted with a cheerful good-bye.

So ended Sissy's first day at TenHuis Chocolade.

That summer, Joe and I had been sitting out in the yard after dinner every evening. We had a reason besides just enjoying the twilight; a great horned owl had shown up in the neighborhood, and if we sat out there, covered with mosquito repellent and talking quietly, we usually saw her glide silently along over our lane. We knew the owl was a she because Joe had spotted her nest in a hollow in one of our maples. Using binoculars, we'd seen the giant owlet the nest had held, and we'd even seen the young owl take one of its first flights.

According to the bird book, a great horned owl has a wingspread of fifty-five inches. That's about four and a half feet. This was one big bird. She preyed on field mice and other small rodents, so she was a very nice bird to have visiting our yard. But she was

71

so huge and so silent that I had an irrational feeling she might carry off one of us.

I don't claim to be a major nature lover, but that owl was awesome.

Having a quiet talk about the day's happenings with your husband can be awesome, too. And that night, as we waited for the owl, I reported to Joe on Sissy's first day on the job.

"Sissy seems like a good worker, and she's eager to get into the swing of things. I just hope all this interest in her dies down. It may increase business, but the gawkers and gossips are a pain in the neck."

"Of course, you were a bit curious about Sissy yourself."

"True. I admit I gawked at her that first day I met her in the supermarket. But now I'm curious about someone else — Wildflower."

"Sissy's grandmother? I haven't seen her around town that I know of. I hear she's almost a recluse."

"I'd love to meet her."

"Why?"

"Because everybody says she's a hippie. I thought all the hippies became regular citizens twenty years before I was born. I read about them, and I guess I always had a sneaking wish that I'd been around to be one."

"A hippie? But, Lee, you're an accountant."

"Even accountants might like to kick over the traces a little. The idea of having long flowing hair, of sitting around while singing folk songs, of living in a commune, of demonstrating for justice — it has a romantic feel."

"Well, you have long hair and you can sing folk songs, and I think you're in favor of justice, but I definitely don't see you in a commune. You like your privacy."

"True. Still, I'd like to meet Wildflower."

Joe looked serious. "I guess you could just go out to Moose Lodge and introduce yourself."

"Oh yeah. 'Hi there, hippie. I'd like to stare at you.' I don't think so."

"You could ask Sissy to introduce you."

"She said she would sometime, but I'll have to wait until it's convenient, and you said yourself that Wildflower doesn't come to town often. I can't think of any excuse to just go out there and introduce myself."

"Excuse?" Joe thought a moment. "Well, you could join a church and say you were recruiting new members."

I rolled my eyes.

"You could support a political campaign and canvass for votes. Or ask Wildflower to join the Warner Pier Chamber of Commerce. Or to contribute to the Red Cross."

"Or I could forget the whole thing, and sometime Wildflower will come by to have lunch with Sissy, and I'll meet her."

Joe punched the air with his fist. "Be proactive, Lee. Wildflower is a taxidermist. You could take a dead animal out there to be stuffed."

"Sure. Next time I see a roadkill raccoon, I'll shovel it into the back of the van. I'm sure Wildflower would love that."

I'm sorry to report that was almost what happened.

CHAPTER 6

That evening was the final time we saw our beautiful great horned owl. The next morning Joe saw an odd lump of fluffy brown out under a tree, the one where she often roosted during the day. When he investigated, he found her lying in the bushes, dead.

He called me, and the two of us stood over her.

"Oh, gee," I said. "I wonder what happened to her."

"I don't see any signs of injury," Joe said. "I guess birds die just the way other creatures do."

She looked much smaller, lying in the bushes where she had fallen. With her broad wings furled, she was no longer a giant. As the bird book said, she was only twenty-two inches or so long from the tips of her tail feathers to the tops of her feathery horns. It had been her huge wingspread that made her seem so large.

Joe pushed back the sleeve of his lawyer suit and checked the time. "I have to leave. We can put her in a garbage bag, and I'll bury her this evening."

I smiled, but it wasn't a happy smile. "The last time I held a funeral for a dead bird it was a sparrow, and I was six years old."

"I was seven, I think. But I don't want to just toss her away. She's been a pal."

"I'll call someone from the bird club and see if there's a scientific use for a dead bird."

"Donate her body to science? That sounds good."

Our evenings weren't going to be the same without the big bird swooping by.

After Joe left, I called the president of the Warner Pier Bird Club. He directed me to the biology department at one of the colleges in Kalamazoo, sixty miles away. He said they had a collection of mounted birds and animals. I called them at eight thirty. I talked to one of the biology professors, asking if they'd like a great horned owl corpse.

"Hmmm," he said. "You're at Warner Pier? Can you freeze it?"

"I don't have freezer space for something this big."

"The problem would be getting someone over there to pick it up in a timely manner."

I considered my schedule. I had an important customer coming by at one o'clock, and it was an hour's drive from Warner Pier to Kalamazoo. "I'll bring it, but I can't come until tomorrow. Maybe I can find freezer space for it."

"Wait a minute! There's someone there who could help out. Do you know where the Moose Lodge Taxidermy place is?"

"Sure."

"Ms. Hill does scientific mounting for us. Give her a ring. If you can get it to her, she can look the owl over and call the collection curator if she thinks it's a good specimen."

I hung up, shaking my head. Joe's joking suggestion that I take Wildflower a dead animal had come true. But I hated taking her a friend.

A quick phone call to Moose Lodge Taxidermy was answered, not by Wildflower but by Sissy. She checked with her grandmother and assured me the older woman planned to be in her shop all morning. And, yes, she'd look the owl over. If it was a good specimen, she'd either mount the owl or prepare it as a study skin for the college.

"I could just take it home with me tonight," Sissy said, "but it ought to be refrigerated in the meantime."

"That's going to be hard to do. This is a

big sucker. I'll take it out there as soon as I get the shop open. Tell your grandmother I'll be there as quickly as possible. With the big bird in a bag."

"She says to make sure it's dead. Some guy once brought her a duck he'd shot, and when he opened the trunk of his car to get it out, the thing flew off. Scared him half to death."

I lifted the sack holding the owl into the back of my van. The bird was surprisingly light. I remembered being told that the bones of birds are hollow, plus a lot of the owl's bulk was feathers. I guess birds can't weigh much or they couldn't fly.

Getting the shop open and telling Aunt Nettie where I was going took only a few minutes. Explaining the day's tasks to Sissy, a brand-new employee, took a little longer. But by ten a.m. I was back in the van and headed east along the two-lane state highway that went past Moose Lodge Taxidermy.

I got more nervous by the mile. First, I was going to meet Wildflower. Second, I had to pass through the scariest kind of Michigan terrain to do it.

I guess if I live up here in Michigan until I'm a hundred, I'll still be a plains person. Not being able to see the horizon makes me uneasy, and the highway leading east out of

Warner Pier is just a narrow cut between trees that grow from sixty to a hundred feet high.

It's like the story about the Texas boy who took a trip to the big woods of Minnesota. When he came back, someone asked him if he had seen a lot of pretty country. He shook his head. "I didn't see a thing," he said. "No matter which way I looked, trees were blocking the view."

Folks from Prairie Creek, in North Texas, don't see what's funny about that story.

But I drove on anyway, into the woods and undergrowth, into country where the trees grew right down to the edges of the highway, into places where the bushes and vines and weeds were so thick that walking among the trees would be impossible.

When I turned at the professionally lettered Taxidermy sign, I found myself even closer to the trees. A narrow sandy lane led past the ramshackle little wooden stand Aunt Nettie said had once been used to sell tomatoes and strawberries and past the rustic sign that read MOOSE LODGE. That sign was decorated with a cartoonish moose with a goofy expression. It needed painting.

The undergrowth was thick next to the highway, but, after about fifty feet, the vegetation suddenly cleared out. The property became open and sunny, with only an occasional tree. The thick growth near the road was used to create privacy, I realized.

Once I was in the cleared area, I saw three buildings — two small houses and, farther back, a building that looked like a metal barn. The houses were both covered with rough siding; they weren't log cabins, but they had that feeling. They had been left unpainted. They had porches across the front. Originally, I deduced, they'd both been the same size, but one now had an ell on one side. Both buildings had stone chimneys. Both looked neat and trim, with small, tidy yards. Both yards were fenced.

As Hogan had said, the dwellings were far from shacks. They were simply deliberately rustic. The only thing ramshackle was the old fruit stand out by the road.

Sissy had told me her grandmother would be back in "the shop," and I assumed that was the metal building. I drove past the houses, pulled onto a gravel parking area, and got out of the van, giving a quick toot on the horn. I got the owl out of the rear deck and headed toward the door.

Entering the building was like ducking underwater. Fish were swimming all around everywhere.

The fish — most of them were huge —

swam over all the walls and hung from the ceiling.

Then I looked farther into the room, and I saw the birds. Ducks, geese, quail, and wild turkeys were suspended like mobiles, and a few were taking flight from the floor.

Next I spotted the animals. An opossum swung from a branch hung on the wall, and a raccoon sat beside an acrylic pool and washed its food. A black squirrel was on top of a display case, beside the telephone.

The startling thing was that I didn't feel as though I'd walked into an exhibit of stuffed animals. These were so lifelike that I felt as if I had walked into a pen full of live animals, birds, and fish. The fish seemed to swish their tails, the birds might have waggled their wings any moment, and the small critters had eyes that looked back at me just the way I was looking at them. None of them moved, but I wouldn't have been surprised if they had.

If these were examples of Wildflower's work, she was a true expert.

There wasn't a sound in the room. It took me a minute to absorb all this. Then I called out. "Hello!"

"Hello!" A voice came from an inner room. "I'm back here."

I went through an open door and found

myself in a large workshop. At the back, standing beside a large metal table with a rim around it, was a gray-haired woman.

I had finally met Wildflower, Warner Pier's last remaining hippie. She was skinning an enormous fish.

"Sorry about the aroma," she said. "A fish is always a fish. You got here a little sooner than I expected."

"What is that you're working on? It's huge!"

"A muskie. The dream fish of Michigan anglers. This guy weighed about forty-five pounds."

"Wow!"

"Wow is right. The Michigan record is just over fifty pounds, so he's a biggie. A Chicago man caught him up north."

I watched as Wildflower expertly removed the thick, fatty skin from the fish.

"It seems too bad that nobody will eat that huge fish," I said.

"Muskies are good eating, true, but that Chicago guy will have more fun showing it off. Actually, I'll freeze some filets for him." Wildflower smiled. "And Sissy and I may have a fish dinner. I'll look at your bird in a minute."

"No hurry. As long as I'm back by one o'clock, I'm fine."

"Good. Maybe you'll have time for a cup of coffee."

Wildflower gave me a quick look from under her eyelashes, and I realized something. While I'd been dying to get a look at Wildflower, she'd been dying to get a look at me. That was natural enough. Her granddaughter was working for me, after all.

"Sure," I said. "I never turn down a cup of coffee."

I watched for about five minutes, studying Wildflower while she finished skinning the fish. She was built nothing like Sissy. Where Sissy was petite, her grandmother was tall and on the skinny side. Wildflower had long gray hair — as a hippie should — and it hung down her back in a loose braid. A bright red twisty, the sort found on a bread package, was wound around the end of the braid, and she was wearing tattered jeans and a baggy T-shirt. Her skin was wrinkled and leathery, like the skin of a person who spent a lot of time outdoors and couldn't be bothered with a hat.

Her hands were fascinating. They had long graceful fingers, the kind people call surgeon's or pianist's hands. Their movements were graceful, as well as quick and deft.

"Your work is beautiful," I said. "The possum out front nearly bit me."

Wildflower laughed. "He's usually pretty docile. I mount only small animals, fish, and birds. No deer, sailfish, or lions."

"You must have a successful operation if you can limit your clientele that way."

"In this part of Michigan, my business would be mostly fish anyway, with birds through the fall and winter. It's only the deer hunters and the guys who go to Africa that I have to turn away."

The room we were in was about thirty feet long and twenty feet wide. About half of it was filled with metal shelving, and that shelving was packed with cans and jars. Among them I saw a box labeled BORAX DECAHYDRATE — Wildflower said it was close to an old-fashioned product called 20 Mule Team Borax — a camp fuel similar to kerosene, and a gallon bottle of Elmer's Wood Glue. The big metal table had a drain and hot and cold running water. This, she said, was actually an autopsy table she picked up at a sale of surplus medical equipment. Midway along one side of the shop was a huge commercial freezer.

The accountant in me toted up the equipment in the shop. Hmmm. Wildflower couldn't be as hard up as Warner Pier people thought she was. Her property, buildings, and equipment would be worth quite a bit. Of course, that could all be countered by debt, but somehow that didn't seem likely.

In a few minutes she hung up the fish skin on a hook and cleaned out her work area. She looked at my owl and pronounced it a beautiful specimen. Then she showed me the other two rooms in the shop. One was a storage room full of what looked like tiny dinosaurs. Wildflower explained that these were Styrofoam forms used as the innards of mounted animals. My mental picture of "stuffing" the wild animals over a wire skeleton had been completely wrong. The other room was a drying room, where mounted fish with blank eyes hung from the ceiling. Wildflower said they were waiting to be embellished with paint and to have their eyes implanted.

"This is fascinating," I said. "Do you give tours?"

"Not formal tours. I run a one-woman business, so I don't have a lot of time for visitors."

"I guess this property is pretty remote. Not like things are along the lakeshore."

"It's not too remote." She gestured toward the back of the shop building. "We have eighty acres, and the Fox Creek Nature Preserve adjoins our property on the north."

"Oh! Joe and I have hiked there. It's beautiful in the spring."

"It draws people year-round. The trails are used by cross-country skiers in the winter, of course, and by hikers the rest of the year." She grinned. "I assure you, we don't have as much privacy as we would like sometimes. So the Warner Pier stories about us running a nudist colony out here are not true. Somebody would have seen my skinny butt."

"I hadn't heard that one!"

"People always come up with creative stories about anybody who doesn't fit the mold. And I broke the mold a lot of years ago. Do you still have time for coffee?"

"Sure."

She led the way to the larger of the two rustic houses, the one with the ell. We entered through a large mudroom that any rural Michigan homeowner would have loved to have. It had a sink for washing dirty hands and muddy boots, a big rubber tray for draining boots, and hooks along the wall for coats. A door led into the kitchen. Beyond that, the living room was visible through a large pass-through.

And way at the end of the living room, hanging on a giant stone fireplace and chimney, was the head of an enormous moose.

I followed Wildflower through the kitchen and realized the living room must be in the ell extension to the house. It was a room about thirty feet long and fifteen feet wide.

The stone fireplace and chimney were beautiful. They were made of light-colored stone, hewn into blocks and laid in an intricate pattern. But the moose head was so gigantic, it dominated the room.

"I thought you didn't do large animals," I said.

"The moose is not my handiwork. It was here when I moved in. A previous owner shot it in Canada. It was pioneer days the last time anybody shot a moose in Michigan."

I knew that Michigan has moose on the Upper Peninsula, but they are protected from hunting.

"I guess the moose head inspired my craft," Wildflower said.

"Oh?"

"When I moved out here nearly fifty years ago with a group of friends, we thought the moose was amusing. One of the girls painted the Moose Lodge sign, and the guys hung the head over the fireplace. After a few years, the thing began to need demothing. I visited a taxidermist to find out how to fix it up myself. I wound up doing a sort of apprenticeship with him. And here I am. The five-thousand-year-old taxidermist." She waved at a couch. "Have a seat."

Wildflower had kept moving as she talked, walking back into the kitchen. Now she was pouring coffee from an electric pot. "Do you take cream?"

I declined and sat down on a long couch at right angles to the fireplace. It was covered with what a decorator would call "throws" and what Aunt Nettie referred to as "afghans." There were three or four of the knitted blankets in wild colors and crazy patterns. They looked perfect in the rustic setting.

All the room's furniture matched the décor of the house. The legs of the end tables were made of branches. A buffalo-skin rug was stretched in front of the fireplace.

"What a comfortable room," I said.

"We like it." Wildflower sat down in a rocking chair that looked as if it had been made from sticks someone found in the woods. She leaned back and sipped her coffee. Then she spoke.

"Well. Do you think you can figure out who killed Buzz?"

CHAPTER 7

I'm surprised I didn't slop coffee all over the afghans.

Instead, I simply stared at her. But she must have known I was startled when I replied to her question.

"I don't intend to fry," I said. "I mean, try! I couldn't figure out who killed anybody. That's a job for the authorities."

"I don't trust the authorities." Wildflower shrugged. "I guess I never have trusted authorities of any sort. And that sheriff thinks Sissy killed Buzz."

"Hogan Jones doesn't think that." I knew Wildflower would know that my aunt was married to the police chief; she didn't live in Warner Pier, but she got her mail there.

Wildflower didn't reply right away. She let the silence grow before she spoke.

"This is the room where Buzz was found," she said. "He was lying in front of the fireplace."

"It must have been awful."

Wildflower shrugged. "I put down a different rug. The *authorities* kept the old one. But Sissy and I decided we'd better keep using the room. We thought that would recapture the atmosphere it always had."

"I'm sure that was wise. And the room has a comfortable, homey atmosphere."

She smiled, and I sipped my coffee, formulating another comment on the room. But before I could speak, Wildflower burst out again.

"Sissy has an alibi for that morning, but it's only me. I'm the only one who can back up what she says. A grandma's testimony won't cut much ice with the cops."

I started to tell Wildflower that Sissy's alibi checked out with people who had seen her in Holland the morning Buzz died. Then I decided I'd better not blab what Hogan had told me. But I remembered that Sissy had consulted Joe's poverty law agency about legal help with her custody case.

"If Sissy needs help," I said, "Joe's agency can link her up with a defense attorney."

Wildflower's face grew contemptuous. "An attorney?" She sounded as if I had suggested she consult an ax murderer. "I hope it doesn't come to that."

Before I could reply, she went on. "Sissy

shouldn't have gone to your husband's agency. But that doesn't matter. The reason I'm asking if you're interested in the case is that you — well, you have a reputation for figuring things out."

"I've stumbled over things. But I'm not as knowledgeable as a professional investigator. I might do more harm than good. If you want an independent investigation of Buzz's death, you need to hire a special investigator."

Wildflower sipped her coffee again. When she spoke, she went to a different topic.

"How'd you meet that lawyer you married?" She was still managing to give the word "lawyer" an extra layer of meaning, and it wasn't a complimentary definition.

I ignored her tone and explained that Joe had been a lifeguard at Warner Pier Beach when I was a teenaged employee at TenHuis Chocolade, so I had known who he was from the time I was sixteen. But we didn't get acquainted until we were thirtyish. I left out the part about the stupid first marriages each of us had made in the meantime. Then I asked Wildflower where she was from originally. Her answer was Detroit. Neither of us referred to Buzz's death again. The conversation continued along conventional lines, though her comments weren't always conventional. I saw where Sissy got her habit of making blunt remarks.

By the time I left, I had attained my goal, and I thought Wildflower had, too. We each got a look at someone who was part of Sissy's life. Despite any talk around Warner Pier, Wildflower didn't seem too odd to me — just blunt. I hoped I didn't seem too odd to her. I probably just seemed ditsy, thanks to my typical slip of the tongue.

I didn't stay long. After all, Wildflower had a bird to skin, and I had a client coming. As I drove back to Warner Pier, my mind ranged back to her original question. "Do you think you can figure out who killed Buzz?"

I had immediately denied any intention of even trying to do that. Had I been honest? I long ago admitted I was the nosiest person around. Had I gotten interested in Sissy because of the mystery in her life?

No, I told myself firmly.

Buzz had probably been killed by some ordinary intruder, by a burglar who broke into Wildflower's house, thinking it was empty. I had no reason to get involved in a case like that. That required the expertise of professional detectives.

I wasn't interested in Buzz's death, I told myself smugly. Instead, I made myself wonder why Wildflower distrusted lawyers. She hadn't wanted Sissy to consult one even when her father-in-law tried to gain custody of her son. Buzz's death was a tragedy to Sissy and Wildflower, and for little Johnny. But it was none of my business.

Until ten o'clock that night I was convinced I had no interest in Sissy except as an employee. That was when Joe and I heard the chug-chug of a Volkswagen as it drove down our lane.

We looked at each other. That lane didn't serve any house but ours.

"Kind of late for a caller," Joe said.

The chugging stopped, and running footsteps pounded across the porch. Someone banged on the door. There was yelling. "Lee! Joe!"

I jumped up. "It's Sissy!"

Joe and I both rushed to the door. He threw it open, and Sissy almost fell in.

"Oh Lordy, Joe! I need a lawyer bad!"

"What's happened?"

"Helen Ferguson is dead, and that idiot sheriff is sure to think I killed her!"

That certainly got me out of the mood for going to bed. What had happened?

It took a few minutes to get Sissy coherent enough to tell us what was going on.

Ace Smith's housekeeper, the tarted-up,

middle-aged blonde who had come into the shop the day before, was lying dead at Beech Tree Beach, just a short way from our house. Sissy had stumbled over her body at the bottom of the steps that led down to the beach. No, Sissy hadn't yet called the authorities.

"My phone won't work out on the lake-shore," she said. "This was the closest place I could think of to come."

"Lee, you call 9-1-1." Joe headed for the kitchen drawer where we keep the flash-lights. "Get the cops and an ambulance. I'll go down there and see if she's really dead."

"Oh, she's dead," Sissy said. "Her head! No live woman ever held her head at that angle."

I argued vaguely with Joe. I hated for him to go down to that beach — which had no lighting — if a killer might be lurking around. He ignored me.

But before he went out the door, he turned to Sissy. "Were there any cars around at the beach?" he asked.

"Just Helen's."

"Did you see anybody else there?"

Sissy shook her head. "I — I don't think so."

"Why did you go there, anyway?"

"Helen said she had something to tell me.

94

She sent me a text message."

"Call 9-1-1," Joe told me firmly. "Then call Hogan. And you and Sissy stay here."

I obeyed, mainly because I didn't have a better idea. I couldn't leave Sissy alone, and it would have taken a forklift to get her back to that beach.

Within five minutes of my 9-1-1 call I heard the first siren. It sounded beautiful.

Sissy was so upset that I didn't ask her any questions, and she didn't volunteer any more of her story.

But I had a bunch of questions waiting, such as why on earth she had gone to Beech Tree Beach in the dark, even if Helen asked her to come. Why would she agree to meet someone when they'd publicly exchanged harsh words the day before?

After about half an hour, a state cop, a woman, came to the door. She'd been sent to stay with us, she said. She didn't explain just why, but Sissy looked crushed.

"I'm not going anywhere," she said.

Sissy had, of course, called Wildflower to tell her she wouldn't be home right away. Her son was sleeping peacefully, she reported.

Soon after the state cop came, Joe returned. "I was just in the way down there," he said.

Sissy clasped her hands imploringly, or maybe she was wringing them. "Helen really is dead?"

Joe nodded.

"I was sure she was," Sissy said dully.

"At least we're inside the city limits," Joe said.

"What does that mean?"

"It means the sheriff won't be involved."

"Oh." That didn't seem to comfort Sissy. She sank into a seat at the end of the couch. "This is such a nightmare."

Joe sat down on the coffee table, facing her. "Sissy, do you want me to call someone to represent you?"

"Represent me?"

"A lawyer, Sissy."

"I didn't kill her, Joe."

"I understand. But you still might need a lawyer."

"I don't have any money."

"That can be worked out."

Sissy rested her head on her hand. "Don't call anybody yet."

"Sissy, you need to get hold of yourself," Joe said. "It's too soon to panic."

"Why? When Buzz died, everybody thought I did it. And I loved Buzz. I didn't even like Helen."

Joe stopped her with a gesture. "Buzz was

shot. Helen Ferguson wasn't. She may have fallen down those stairs. Don't panic until there's an official cause of death. It could have been an accident."

Joe's words seemed to get through to Sissy. She sat up and gulped. "I guess finding her like that just brought back the whole nightmare with Buzz. I'll try to act braver."

I went to the kitchen to make a large pot of coffee. In a few minutes Joe joined me. We muttered together over the sink.

"Do you really think there's a possibility Helen Ferguson was killed in an accident?" I said.

"I don't like coincidences. But maybe I'm being cynical. I'm not a medical examiner."

"Coincidences? What's coincidental about Helen's death?"

"Sissy's a murder suspect to the Warner Pier community. She has a fight with Helen. Helen texts Sissy — *texts*, Lee. It's not a form of communication that requires direct communication. She asks Sissy to meet her. She's dead when Sissy gets there. It's too squirrelly for me."

I just nodded. "I wish you weren't right, but I'm afraid you are."

More headlights flashed on the trees in our yard. "More cops," I said. "I'm beginning to regard the *authorities* the way

97

Wildflower does."

This car also parked out on the lane, where quite a traffic jam must have been developing. Joe and I went back into the living room. But when Joe opened the door, the voice I heard didn't sound authoritative. It sounded almost timid.

"Hi. I'm Chip Smith. I'm a cousin of Sissy's. Sort of. By marriage. One of the cops said she was over here. Can I see her?"

Joe stepped back, and Chip came in, all six-feet-plus of handsomeness and personality. I could feel the drool forming under my tongue. He sure was a fine physical specimen.

Sissy jumped to her feet. "Chip!"

Chip grinned his crooked grin. "Hi, Sissy. I wanted to see if you needed any help."

He walked toward her and opened his arms wide, offering her a big hug.

Sissy raised both hands, holding them with the palms toward him.

"You jerk! Will you leave me alone? The last thing I need at this particular moment is you."

Chip did not get the hug he'd aimed for. Instead, Sissy shoved him away. She didn't seem to push him very hard, but he stumbled backward. He fell against the mantel. The fireplace screen went over, and all the tools clattered onto the brick hearth.

CHAPTER 8

For a moment I thought Chip was going to land on the floor in the middle of the fire tools, but Joe — the natural athlete — caught him and kept him upright.

The whole thing made such a crash that I thought Chip must have been injured. I guess Sissy did, too, because she gasped out a question. "Are you hurt?"

"No, I'm okay. Sorry to be so clumsy."

Sissy stepped forward and took Chip's arm. She led him into the dining room and turned her back to Joe, the state trooper, and me.

If she was looking for privacy, of course she didn't get it. She and Chip were just around fifteen feet from us, and we could hear every word they said.

"Now listen, Chip. You were Buzz's best friend, as well as his cousin, and I know you were important to him. I want to be friends with you. Friends! But this is not a good time."

"Sissy . . ."

"I'm not kidding, Chip. The Warner Pier gossip mill has me down as a murderess, thanks to Helen and Ace. Now Ace is trying to get custody of Johnny. The last thing I need is for people to think I've taken up with my husband's cousin and best friend just five months after he died."

"Come on, Sissy. No one who knows you could —"

"Most people don't know me personally. They go by what they hear. Don't be naive, Chip! Maybe we could see each other, as friends, a year or two down the road, after Ace and I have settled our problems. After the cops — please God! — have arrested some tramp or other for Buzz's murder, then we can be friends again. But right now, please get out of my life!"

She stalked back into the living room and dropped into a chair — not the couch. Sissy wasn't giving Chip a chance to sit beside her.

Even after that, Chip argued that his only goal was to protect Sissy. She ignored him, and Joe told him he'd better leave. He finally did.

After Chip was out the door, Joe made a feeble joke. "That guy doesn't seem to speak English very well."

Sissy held her head in her hands. "He's unbelievable. He has a reputation among his friends as quite a ladies' man. I guess no woman ever turned him down before."

"Well, you've got witnesses," I said.

"I might need them." Sissy shot a glance at the state cop, now sitting quietly in a chair against the wall.

"Did you ever go out with him?"

"No! I've never been alone with him in my life. Unless he came by to see Buzz and had to wait on him or something. Now he's bringing me flowers?"

"Maybe he thinks he has to make a move before anybody else does," I said.

"Nobody has shown any interest in me." Sissy shook her head. "I've always tried to be nice to Chip because Buzz liked him. When Ace sent Buzz away to military school, Chip was there, too. He was a year ahead of Buzz, and I guess he really helped him out. Stood up for him. But Chip's never been my favorite person. He sucks up to Ace too much."

I handed coffee around then, and we waited. After about a half hour, another car came. This one edged past the cars sitting in the lane and went around to the back, where Joe and I and our visitors normally park.

Joe looked out the kitchen window. "It's Hogan," he said. "They must be nearly finished down at the beach."

Hogan came in and accepted a cup of coffee; then he sat down opposite Sissy.

"I know you're exhausted," he said, "but I have to get a preliminary statement. Then you can go home."

Sissy looked relieved. I took myself off to the dining room, but Hogan didn't tell me to go into another part of the house, so I didn't. Joe kept his seat near Sissy. Though he doesn't do criminal law, Sissy had consulted him. I could almost see him thinking he'd better stick with her, even if his status was informal.

Hogan's questions weren't onerous. He just got Sissy to tell her story. There was no way I couldn't hear the interview.

Sissy said she'd received a text message from Helen Ferguson at about seven thirty p.m. She showed her cell phone to Hogan, and he read the message out loud.

" 'Sissy! I've stumbled across something crazy about Ace. It ought to stop him trying to take Johnny away from you. You need to know this! Meet me at Beech Tree Beach at ten o'clock, and I'll tell you. Don't bring anybody. If Ace finds out I've blabbed, I'll be in trouble.' "

Hogan put the phone down on the coffee table. "I'll have to keep your phone for a while, Sissy. Had you ever received a text message from Helen before?"

"No! In fact, back when I saw Helen occasionally — before Buzz died — when Ace and I were still speaking — she told me she didn't know how to use the text feature of her phone. She was sort of proud about it."

"Yeah, us old folks don't trust technology. Did you have any doubt that the message was from Helen?"

"Not really. Of course, she'd used the one bait I couldn't resist. I'd do anything to get rid of Ace's threat to take Johnny away from me."

"I understand."

"I talked to my grandmother, and we agreed that I should go. Helen was in a position to know a lot about Ace, and I couldn't miss a chance at learning something that would help me end this custody battle. So I gave Johnny his bath and read him a story. He went off to sleep long before I left the house."

"When did you leave?"

"About nine fifteen."

"What time did you get to the beach?"

"Maybe ten minutes to ten. Helen's car was in the parking lot. I guess it's still there."

"We towed it," Hogan said. "Did you go straight down to the beach?"

"I went straight to the stairs. Since Helen's car was there, I thought she was, too." Sissy took two deep breaths before she went on. "I stopped at the top of the stairs and called to her. Then I flashed my flashlight around. Helen was lying in the sand at the foot of the stairs."

"Did you go down to her?"

"Oh, yes! I thought maybe I could help her. But I couldn't find a pulse. And her hand was limp when I touched it. When I saw the angle of her head" — Sissy held a tissue to her mouth and blinked rapidly — "I was careful not to move her."

"Did you call the cops right away?"

"I tried. But my cell phone didn't have any service, so I thought of Lee and Joe."

"How did you know where they live?"

"Somebody told me. Lee? Maybe Lee mentioned it. Or somebody told me they lived right across Lake Shore Drive from the Garretts. Dick Garrett brought a big fish out for my grandmother to mount."

"There are houses closer to the beach. Did you think of going to one of them?"

"I was afraid to. I mean — well, I was

scared."

"Why? Did you think Helen hadn't had an accident?"

"I didn't know what had happened to her. I guess I was scared because — well, partly it was all this gossip, I guess. You know, people thinking I killed Buzz. And here I'd found a body. I didn't want it all to get started again."

"I can understand that, Sissy. I can understand that fear making you run away, maybe denying you'd found Mrs. Ferguson's body. But why would that make you afraid to go to the closest house?"

Sissy's head drooped. "You'll think it was stupid."

"Try me."

"I know it was just my imagination running away with me."

"Try me."

Sissy sighed again and looked at Joe. He nodded encouragingly.

She burst out suddenly. "I thought there was somebody on the beach!"

Hogan blinked solemnly. "Well, it's a public beach."

"I know! But this guy just stood there. I thought he was watching me."

"Did you speak? Call out?"

"Yes. I yelled, 'Help!' But he didn't come

toward me. He sort of faded into the trees over on the left. I got scared! I dropped Helen's hand, and I ran back up the stairs, and I jumped in the car and locked the doors."

Her face looked agonized. "And now I'm not even sure there was anybody there! But after that, I was afraid to go to a strange house. I came here because I didn't think Joe and Lee were likely to kill me! I ran off and left poor Helen lying there because I was scared, and maybe I could have helped her!"

I wanted to give Sissy a big Texas hug and tell her not to blame herself. That must have been a terrifying experience. Who could have been there, lurking in the dark? I wondered if Hogan and his crew had found any trace of the person. Or had it been Sissy's imagination? At any rate, she didn't need to feel guilty about running for help.

Hogan nodded reassuringly. "At that point, Sissy, I'm sure there was nothing to be done for Helen, so you don't need to beat yourself up over leaving her."

She reached for a tissue. "I know. I'm sure she was already dead. I just hate to admit I was such a coward."

"Running away from a man who hangs back in the shadows — after you've just found a body — doesn't seem cowardly to me. It sounds smart."

"But I wasn't sure there was anybody there." She looked at Hogan. "Did you find any tracks?"

"We'll have to look again in the daylight. Now, Sissy, I'd like to keep your car until tomorrow. Joe? Can you and Lee take Sissy home?"

We agreed, of course. We all piled into Joe's truck, even though we had to sit three abreast. At least nobody had to crane his neck to talk.

"I can't believe Chief Jones doesn't think I'm involved in Helen's death in some way," Sissy said.

"Lawyers are taught to be cautious, and we try to get that across to our clients," Joe said. "So I'm going to warn you to be careful when you talk to Hogan again."

"He doesn't seem to think I had anything to do with it, Joe."

"He doesn't have a cause of death yet."

"What do you mean?"

"I mean the medical examiner hasn't looked at Helen's body. He should be able to tell if she was really killed by a fall down those stairs, or . . ." Joe paused. "Or if there was some other factor."

"What else could have happened?"

"Just as an example, somebody could have

108

killed her elsewhere, then brought her body there and tossed it down the stairs. Somebody could have pushed her down them, then broken her neck manually. Hogan doesn't even know the time of death yet."

"Surely she hadn't been dead very long when I got there. Her hand was warm when I touched it."

"They'll have to check the body temperature, the stomach contents. A bunch of stuff. So, Sissy, speaking as your lawyer — sort of — be careful. None of these carefree remarks you tend to make."

"You mean, like pointing out what a pain in the neck Helen was, and that I thought she was the main source of gossip about me?"

Joe shook a finger. "That never happened. Okay? If someone asks you specifically, don't lie. But you don't have to volunteer information."

"Okay." Sissy's voice sounded subdued. "But I sure wonder what Helen wanted to tell me about Ace."

I wondered about that, too. After all, Ace could be a prime suspect in her death. If he discovered that she had some sort of evidence against him, something that would stop him from getting custody of Johnny — even linking him to Buzz's death — well, it would sure be logical for him to take steps to shut her up.

It was hard to picture Ace killing his own son.

But it was not impossible. I'd been around detectives enough to know that the people closest to the victim — spouse, parents, brother, sister, friends — are considered the obvious suspects. And certainly Ace and Buzz had apparently been at odds for years. They'd quarreled about Buzz's career choices, about his marriage to Sissy, probably about other things. Maybe their disagreements had grown from name calling to violence.

Sissy was silent until we neared the turn into Moose Lodge's drive.

Wildflower had obviously turned on all the lights, because the place was ablaze with electricity. I once again marveled at the view Warner Pier had of Wildflower and Sissy. They were believed to be poverty stricken, but Wildflower's home was comfortable, if not luxurious, and all those lights had cost a mint to install.

Wildflower had heard us coming, of course, and she was standing on the porch of the larger cabin. And there were two people with her, a man and a woman.

"Oh, damn," Sissy said. "Nosy and Rosy

are there. They can scent trouble a mile away. And if there isn't any around, they bring it with them."

CHAPTER 9

The two people with Wildflower were both short and round, and both had white hair. The woman's hair was short and wavy, and the man had a bald pate with a fluffy halo.

After Sissy got out of the truck, Joe would have driven off immediately, but Wildflower motioned to us, so we both got out. I recalled Wildflower's remark about Joe — saying it had been a mistake for Sissy to consult him — so I didn't know what to expect. She apparently had a very poor opinion of lawyers in general and might even object to Joe in particular.

She hugged Sissy and answered her questions about Johnny. "He's sleeping like an angel," she said. "Tiptoe in and take a look."

She watched Sissy go into the house, then turned to us. "I'd like to introduce our closest neighbors, Roosevelt and Nona Reagan."

Hmmm. So "Rosy" was the man, and

"Nosy" was the wife. We all shook hands and made polite noises. I pulled my jacket around me. July nights can be cool in west Michigan.

Wildflower spoke again. "Thank you for helping Sissy tonight."

"We weren't much help," Joe said. "She may need a criminal lawyer. Our agency deals only with noncriminal matters. If money is a problem —"

"Honestly!" The interjection came from Nona Reagan. "How anybody could suspect Sissy of being involved in another death! It's just ridiculous! That girl is the sweetest thing who ever lived. And that little boy is the apple of her eye. All she cares about is taking proper care of him."

I had the impression that she was going to keep talking indefinitely, but when she paused to take a breath, Joe cut her off at the pass. "Right now, Helen Ferguson's death looks to have been accidental," he said. "I'm hoping Sissy won't be involved any further."

Nona's words stopped abruptly, and she stood there with her mouth open. She looked disappointed. Having prepared herself to protect Sissy, she evidently didn't want to hear that Sissy might not need her protection.

Wildflower followed up on Joe's remark as smooth as silk. "I'm going to try to get Sissy right to bed," she said. "Nona, Rosy, I do appreciate your coming over. And I'll talk to you tomorrow."

"We just wanted to warn you, Wildflower. You remember that we had this problem right before Buzz was killed."

"I understand." Was there an ironic undertone to the words? I couldn't tell. In fact, I was quite surprised by Wildflower's behavior. Where was the blunt speech she'd used that morning?

Rosy Reagan shook hands with Joe again. "I try to keep an eye on these girls," he said. "It makes me nervous for the two of them to be living out here all alone."

"We're not too helpless," Wildflower said. This time there was a definite edge to her comment.

"Oh, I know! I know! But it's pretty remote out here." Rosy leaned close to Joe and lowered his voice. "And she's antigun, you know. Won't even keep a pistol for protection."

"Rosy, go home!" Wildflower spoke firmly. "We've been over that a dozen times. Sissy and I will be cautious, but we don't need a gun. And now I have to ask Joe and Lee just one question."

I thought Nosy and Rosy — I was thinking of them that way already — were going to insist on staying to hear what that question was. But they finally started down the porch steps. Each was carrying a large flashlight. They walked off toward the east, both still talking. Apparently they lived close enough to walk over.

Wildflower led us into the house. "I hope Nosy and Rosy don't ever try to sneak up on anyone. The continual rumble of conversation would tip their quarry off. But they're right about one thing. When you live out like we do, you have to be alert to what's going on with your neighbors, as well as with yourself."

"How did they hear about Helen Ferguson?"

"They were already here when Sissy called. They insisted on staying to 'help' me."

"Oh, dear!" I said.

"I didn't discourage them. I was afraid I'd need to leave, to go to Sissy's rescue. And in that case, they would have been willing to stay with Johnny. But they originally came over for quite a different reason."

She lowered her voice. "I don't want Sissy to know about it just yet."

"What happened?"

"Nosy and Rosy think they had a prowler."

"What happened?"

"Oh, they went to Holland today, and when they came back, they found strange tracks out by their garage. I wouldn't take it very seriously, ordinarily."

"Why not?" Joe asked.

"Because our property and theirs run alongside the Fox Creek Nature Preserve, and people walk along there all the time. Sometimes they stray off the paths. But today . . ." She stopped.

"Why is this time different?"

"I was gone for a while this afternoon, too. When I came back, I thought some things had been moved around. I think somebody came into our house."

"Have you called the police?"

"Certainly not! Nothing seems to be missing."

"Even so, Ms. Hill, breaking in —"

"The door wasn't locked."

"Coming into a house uninvited is still a crime. The police —"

"Out here we're served by that sheriff."

"I understand that you don't like Burt Ramsey, but he could investigate. He could take fingerprints. He could talk to the neighbors."

Wildflower shook her head emphatically.

116

"Nosy and Rosy are the only close neighbors we have."

"Did you tell them you thought you'd had a break-in?"

"No. They'd make way too much of it. I don't want to stir them up when nothing was taken."

"What makes you think anyone came in?"

"Some things have been moved around. For example, I had sorted the mail according to my own method before I left. I stacked it on my desk, and now I think it's in a different order."

"Sissy wouldn't have moved it around?"

"I don't think so. I put her mail on her desk. She doesn't usually look at mine."

"Hey, Grandma." Sissy appeared at a door that apparently led into a hall.

Wildflower put a finger on her lip to signal silence to Joe and me. She dropped it as she turned toward Sissy.

"Yes?"

"Did you take the MasterCard bill from my desk? It doesn't seem to be there."

"No, I didn't look at your desk."

"Well, it needs to go in the mail tomorrow. I mean, today."

Sissy went back through the door. I raised my eyebrows. Joe scowled.

"I definitely think you should report this," he said.

"I guess you're right. I'll call tomorrow."

Joe kept scowling, and Wildflower spoke again. "The county has only one deputy at night. Unless we have someone breaking in right that moment, he's not going to come out until tomorrow anyway."

"You're probably right. Do you want me to go to the sheriff's office with you?"

"Don't you have to go to work in Holland?"

"I could arrange it."

"No. I'm not a wimp. I'll call the sheriff myself."

"All right. But lock your doors and windows, okay?"

Wildflower smiled and promised to secure the house.

As we left, I felt a big bite from my curiosity bug. "If you and Sissy and Johnny all live in this house, what do you use the other house for?"

"Now? For storage, mainly. Sissy and Buzz lived there until he was killed."

"Oh?" I said. "They lived over there, but Buzz was killed in this house?"

"That's right."

"Was it unusual for Buzz to come over here?"

"Not really." Wildflower smiled. "He and I usually ate lunch together. He'd come over to make our sandwiches. As I said, I don't usually lock the house up — certainly I wouldn't lock up if I was just working in the shop. Buzz had the run of the place. He'd come out to the shop and talk, bounce ideas off me."

She blinked rapidly. I realized that Sissy wasn't the only person still grieving for Buzz. Hogan had thought Buzz sponged off Sissy and Wildflower, but Wildflower made the four of them sound as if they'd been a happy little family.

I had to blink a few times, too.

Joe asked Wildflower to show him the things she thought were disturbed by the prowler. She said she couldn't find that anything was gone. Things had simply been moved around.

"Mainly papers," she said. "Joe, do you honestly think we're going to get any interest in this from Burt Ramsey?"

"Maybe not, but you need to get it on the record."

Wildflower didn't look convinced.

Sissy came out at that moment, holding the bill she'd been looking for. "It had fallen over the back of the desk," she said. "I don't know how that could happen."

119

We left Wildflower to tell Sissy they'd had a break-in and went home. As soon as we were off the Moose Lodge property, I asked Joe about the burglary.

"Do you think someone broke in?"

"Hard to tell. Since the main things touched seemed to be papers, it could be the breeze blew things around."

"It doesn't exactly get breezy down among all those trees. Do you think Burt Ramsey will do anything about it?"

"No."

On that discouraging note, we stopped talking. By the time we got home, all the lights and cars were gone from Beech Tree Beach. Helen Ferguson would be gone, too. In our one contact, she hadn't impressed me with her charm and intelligence, but she didn't deserve to fall or be pushed down a set of stairs. And Sissy didn't deserve to be involved in another mysterious death. Or I didn't think she did.

By the time we left Moose Lodge, it had been well after midnight, so I had told Sissy she didn't need to come in the next day, but she said she wanted to. We'd agreed that she and I would come in after lunch. Wildflower said she'd bring her, since Sissy's car was being examined by the state police lab.

Because of this, it was one o'clock when I

120

came in the back door of TenHuis Chocolade and walked into the workroom. I immediately knew something was wrong.

All the hairnet ladies were standing still,
frozen in their places. Some had their hands
clasped imploringly. Certainly no work was
being done.

And the reason was plain. Some man was
yelling.

"You're a slick piece of work! But you're
not fooling anybody!"

The shouts were coming from Sissy's tiny
office. The door was closed, but the noise
was so loud that it was coming right through
the barrier.

"Don't think you're going to get away with
this, you little no-good!"

It was Ace. I was sure of it. Sissy's jerk
father-in-law was lambasting her again.

This time he was doing it in my territory.

By golly, he wasn't going to do that on the
premises of TenHuis Chocolade.

I guess I lost my temper completely. I
hardly remember how I got across the
workroom. I probably knocked four people
out of my way. It was just lucky I wasn't
carrying a gun.

I grabbed the door to Sissy's office and
flung it open. A broad-shouldered man was
leaning over Sissy's desk, punching a finger

toward her.

I took one deep breath; then I cut loose.

"Get out of here!" My yelling was louder than his. "You can't talk to one of my employees that way! Out! Now!"

The man stood rigid, his finger still poking into the air.

"This is unforgettable! I mean, unforgivable!" My tongue had twisted, and I was ranting, and I didn't even care. "Shut up with the stupid remarks and get your fanny out of my business! Just who do you think you are? Besides the biggest jerk in Warner Pier?"

I guess I paused to draw a breath. And in that instant, the man leaning over Sissy's desk turned to face me.

I was nose to nose with Burt Ramsey, sheriff of Warner County.

"Oh," I said. "I thought you were someone else."

Sissy giggled. Then she leaned back in her chair and guffawed. Peal after peal of laughter rang out.

And in a few seconds, I joined in. I had made a complete fool of myself.

Back in the days when I was wire editor for a daily newspaper, one of the hardest parts of the job for me was learning a new computer system. This happened periodically because the computer company stopped supporting the old system or came up with a new one, and we had to "upgrade." Then we all knew we were in for several rough weeks. It may have been worse for me, because I have no interest in computers. I regard them as tools, usually tools designed to make my work harder.

Fortunately, Steve, the editor who trained us all to use these infernal machines, had apprenticed with Job. He was incredibly patient, and he actually liked computers.

I was not nearly so patient. After one ninety-minute session, I spoke to him sharply. "Steve, let's quit for a few minutes! I've got to have some M&Ms."

Steve looked astonished. He was having fun, and the call for a chocolate break seemed to amaze him.

"Come on!" I said. "Don't you understand how much *chocolate* it takes to learn a new computer system?"

Steve's patience and chocolate kept my newspaper career going through fifteen years of technical advances. Please don't tell me chocolate doesn't fight stress!

CHAPTER 10

Sissy and I might be in stitches, but the sheriff was not.

He didn't say anything. After all, what could he say? He just glared at me, then reached over to close the door to the office.

I conquered my laughter enough to speak. "If you think closing that door gives the three of us privacy, you're wrong. I heard every word you were saying to Sissy as I came in from the alley. Every lady in the chocolate shop was listening with both ears."

To my surprise, Sheriff Ramsey blushed. He was a sandy-haired, fair-skinned man, and there was no other word for the redness that came over his face. He blushed.

When he spoke, he mumbled. "I guess I lost my temper."

"I did, too," I said. "I thought you were someone else — a person who had no right to come into my business and make a stir.

All the ladies stopped working."

"I guess they were listening."

"They could hardly miss what was going on."

Ramsey looked even more embarrassed. Without another word, he pivoted and walked out of the office. He went through the shop without turning his head to look right or left, opened the front door, and stepped onto the sidewalk.

I was very happy to see him go. Then I thought of Hogan. Hogan was a friend of mine, as well as a relative. And whether Hogan liked Burt Ramsey or not, he needed to get along with him. If Hogan's stepniece publicly lambasted the county sheriff, it was going to cause Hogan trouble. I didn't want to do that. I wondered if I could head off the situation.

So I followed Ramsey. I didn't catch up with him until he was nearly to the SUV with WARNER COUNTY SHERIFF painted on its door.

"Sheriff Ramsey," I said, "I apologize for yelling at you."

That was as much as I could say. I wasn't sorry for what I'd said, but I was sorry I'd lost my temper. So I apologized for yelling and then stopped talking. I didn't take back what I'd said.

"I don't know why the heck you and your aunt hired that woman," Ramsey said.

"We hired her because we needed a book-keeper."

"You can't tell me she was the only book-keeper available in Warner Pier."

"Of course not." I considered going on about how Sissy needed help fighting gossip, but I decided that more explanation would be unwise. I'd have to quote Hogan, for one thing, and I didn't want to get any further into the middle of a fight between Hogan and Burt Ramsey. So I said, rather lamely, "Sissy had the skills we were looking for."

Ramsey turned toward me then, and I saw he certainly hadn't gotten over his mad. "Skills? Skills like shooting people?"

I hadn't gotten over my mad either, and I remembered that Ramsey hadn't been able to break Sissy's alibi for her husband's death.

"Shooting?" I said. "That's nothing. Any idiot with a trigger finger can shoot a gun. It's Sissy's ability to be in two places at once that attracted me."

"She's tricky enough to pull that one off."

"Listen! I guess you're here because Sissy's grandmother reported a break-in. Joe and I both urged her to call your office and report it. Wildflower didn't want to do that, and if this is the reaction they got, I can certainly understand why."

"Did you believe that break-in junk?"

"That's not the point. Sissy and Wildflower are citizens of this county —"

"Citizens!" Ramsey rolled his eyes. "They've given me more trouble than the rest of the citizens put together!"

Now I was shaking a finger at him. "Whatever they've done, TenHuis Chocolade is a business concern. If you want to give Sissy the third degree, you haul her over to the county seat and question her. With her attorney present! But don't you come into my business and bring the whole place to a standstill over it!"

Ramsey and I faced each other. I was happy to note that I was at least two inches taller than he was, and I took full advantage of my height, staring down my nose at him.

Ramsey swung his car door open. "Okay," he said. "You and your aunt have hired Sissy. By doing that, you've made people think Hogan Jones is taking her under his wing."

"No!"

"Yes! So from now on he can take care of her. I'm washing my hands of Moose Lodge and all its problems. As far as I'm concerned, they're no longer located in Warner County."

He got into the SUV and drove off without looking at me again.

I'm afraid I stomped my foot. I was still mad, but I was beginning to admit to myself that losing my temper had gotten me into a mess.

The last thing I wanted to do was instigate some sort of feud between Hogan and a fellow lawman. I hadn't pictured that happening when I hired Sissy.

I took three deep breaths, still standing on the sidewalk, and told myself to calm down. Then I spoke to myself — out loud. "Now what?"

Aunt Nettie answered my question. I hadn't realized she had followed me out of the shop. "Now? Now I guess we'd better tell Hogan what happened," she said.

I whirled toward her. "Did you hear all that?"

"I only came in for the last part. But Dolly gave me a quick rundown on the early stages."

"I feel like a fool. I lost my temper completely."

"Some things are worth losing your temper over."

"But I may have caused trouble between

Hogan and Ramsey."

Aunt Nettie shook her head. "The trouble was already there. Hogan doesn't say much about Ramsey, but he thinks the man is an idiot. And Ramsey knows it."

I looked inside the shop. There were faces — faces looking out at me. The ladies were still staring, trying to understand just what was going on. "I guess I'd better get to work."

"We'd all better get to work."

"I'll try to call Hogan."

"You may not be able to reach him. He's a bit busy today."

Well, yes. Hogan was investigating Helen Ferguson's death. That ought to keep him occupied most of the day, even if he had called in the Michigan State Police.

I went back into the shop and calmed Sissy while Aunt Nettie shooed the ladies back to work. Sissy had stopped laughing and was blaming herself for the commotion, but I told her she'd done the right thing in reporting the break-in, even if the sheriff didn't respond responsibly. I gave her some routine chores to do; then I went to my office and tried to call Hogan.

He wasn't at the police station, of course, and I didn't want to try his cell phone. I left a message with the police department secretary, asking Hogan to call me. Next I stared at my computer screen, pretended to be deep in thought about some accounting problem, and worried about what to do next. It didn't occur to me that I could do nothing. No, I had to take action.

And I remembered that Wildflower had asked me to investigate Buzz's death. I had said I wasn't capable, and that answer was certainly true.

But since then Sissy and Wildflower had had a break-in, and the sheriff was refusing even to look into it.

Maybe I could investigate well enough to handle a minor break-in, though I was sure Hogan — and Joe — would tell me to keep my nose out of the whole situation.

On the other hand, Sheriff Burt Ramsey was so infuriating . . .

After about fifteen minutes, I closed out the computer, got to my feet, and walked back into the workshop. Aunt Nettie was scooping fondant into her wonderful copper pan, the one she used to make filling for bonbons. She had already lighted the little gas fire in the tripod that held it.

"I'm going out for a while," I said. "I'm not sure how long I'll be gone." She didn't ask me where I was going.

I got in my van and drove straight east,

toward Moose Lodge.

I was there before it occurred to me that Wildflower might not be home. I was relieved to see that there were two cars parked outside the big metal workshop building, a Volkswagen van and a midsized silver sedan with a small rental sticker on the back bumper.

I honked to let Wildflower know she had a second caller; then I went into the showroom area. Once again, I had the sensation of being underwater, with beautiful and lifelike fish swimming over my head.

I called out. "Hello! It's Lee Woodyard."

"Come on back." I went into the workshop and found Wildflower working with a large electric stapler, fastening bands of what looked like foam rubber to an animal form. Her back was toward me, and the face of a raccoon looked at me from under her arm. Its eyes were lively, like the lifelike eyes of the raccoon in the display area. I had an uneasy feeling that the raccoon understood what was going on better than I did.

When I tore my eyes away from the raccoon's gaze and looked around the shop, I saw that Chip Smith was leaning on a worktable, watching her.

Seeing Chip made me feel self-conscious. I remembered only too clearly the fight he and Sissy had had in our living room the previous evening.

Chip first looked dismayed when he saw me. Then his expression changed, and he looked slightly pleased. "Hey!" he said. "Here's somebody who can back up my story."

Wildflower looked around at me, and her expression was as blank as the raccoon's.

"Chip says Sissy is mad at him," she said.

"I'm also under that imposition — I mean, impression!" I said. Darn! My nervousness had been revealed by my twisted tongue. I went on quickly. "I really don't blame her, Chip."

He screwed his face up, looking as if I'd kicked him.

"And acting pitiful won't get you any sympathy from me," I said. "Sissy's in a very difficult situation, and you seem to be making it worse."

"I'm just trying to show her she has a friend."

"She has lots of friends. She has me and my aunt and all the ladies at the shop. And that's enough people to sway public opinion in a town the size of Warner Pier."

"Yes, but I represent the Ace Smith camp, and I want to show her that not everybody thinks she's . . ." His voice trailed off.

Wildflower spoke then, and her voice was sharp. "That not everybody thinks she's a murderess and an unfit mother?"

"No! How could anyone think those things about Sissy?"

"It's amazing what a little gossip can do," Wildflower said.

"That's what Sissy's afraid of," I said. "If she were to go around town with a man, particularly one who was pals with Buzz, it might make people think she's dating again."

Chip shook his head. "I don't want to date her! I just want to show her she's got a friend."

Wildflower whacked the raccoon with three more staples. Then she spoke.

"Your intentions may be good, Chip, but Sissy doesn't need any more talk of any sort right now."

"I thought you raised Sissy with the idea that she should do what she wanted and forget about gossip."

"No, Chip, I raised her with the idea she should do what was right — her idea of right — and not try to please everybody else. That's how you wind up with your ass in a ditch."

Chip looked puzzled.

"Didn't you ever read *Aesop's Fables*?"

134

Wildflower asked. "Remember the one about the man and his son taking their donkey to market? The son rides it, but someone says the father should ride. Then the father rides it, but someone says both should ride. Then they both ride it, but people don't like that either. Finally they rig a pole and carry the animal — again because of what a passerby says. And they drop the ass in a ditch and kill it." She paused, then went on. "You've got to do what you think is right. And sometimes avoiding talk is the right thing to do. We don't live in isolation. You've got to show some sense."

It was quite a scolding, and it left Chip looking properly crestfallen. I felt sorry for him, despite my earlier words. After all, Sissy was a darling girl. Obviously guys were going to be interested in her, even if she did choose not to date at the present time. Chip seemed like a healthy, normal male; it was natural that he wanted to pay attention to her.

"I guess I feel guilty," Chip said. "Buzz was my cousin, as well as my best friend, and I couldn't even get here when he died. I was no help to Sissy then."

"That was because of your job," I said. "Where were you when Buzz died?"

"In the — abroad. Normally Dobermann-

Smith can arrange emergency leave, but I was too far out in the boonies to hear what had happened. Ace couldn't get hold of me. It was a week before I could even call Sissy."

"Since you were cousins, I guess you'd known Buzz your whole life."

"We really didn't know each other well until we went away to school. Then it was us against the world."

"Boarding school must be a traumatic experience."

"Oh, I got to like it. But I'm afraid Buzz never did. He was such a creative guy."

"And now a second person associated with Ace Smith has been killed."

"Associated with Ace?" Chip looked completely blank.

"Helen Ferguson worked for him. And didn't she live on his property?"

"Well, yeah. She cleans for him, and he rents her a little house. It's not as if he socializes with her."

"I had the idea she would have liked to socialize with him."

Chip looked surprised, so I went on. "More gossip."

"I don't think that's true," Chip said. "I mean, I don't know what Helen had in mind, of course, but I've noticed Ace always leaves the house when she comes."

"Still, I'll bet he'll have to answer a lot of questions about her."

"What would he know about a cleaning woman?"

Wildflower shot a significant look at me.

"Since she lived on his property, she was a neighbor. The cops will want to know if she had lots of visitors, if she seemed to need money, if he'd seen her yesterday. I imagine they'll ask you about her, too, if they haven't already."

"Me? Why?"

"You're staying there, aren't you?"

"Yes, but I barely knew the damn woman! She just nosed around once a week. I didn't know her any better than she did" — he gestured at Wildflower — "and even less than Sissy did."

Wildflower's reaction was strange. Her eyes widened; then she ducked her head until she was looking that raccoon directly in the eye.

"I don't know anything about Helen Ferguson," she said.

Then she turned as pink as Burt Ramsey had.

Wildflower was a terrible liar.

CHAPTER 11

Wildflower might have been a terrible liar, and she might have lived an unconventional "hippie" life. But she was also an older woman. I guess both Chip and I had been raised to respect our elders. Neither of us called her on her lie. We chitchatted as if we hadn't noticed her blush.

In a few minutes Chip said he had to leave, which suited me because I didn't want to talk about the break-in in front of him. I stayed in the workroom with the keen-eyed raccoon while Wildflower walked Chip out to his rental car.

Now, I thought as I waited, how do I approach this?

I never decided on an answer to that. When Wildflower came back, I simply burst into speech. "That sheriff is even worse than you said. He's not going to do a thing about your break-in!"

Wildflower shrugged. "I've been at odds

with the law so long that it doesn't surprise me."

"But you're . . ." I quit talking before I added the word "ordinary." I didn't find Wildflower as unconventional as her reputation indicated, but this wasn't the time to go into it. "The first time I came out here, you suggested I might look into Buzz's death."

"The law hasn't done us any good."

"I'm not skilled enough to investigate a murder. But maybe I could collect a little evidence about a burglary."

"Doing something is better than doing nothing."

"Have you got time to talk now?"

"Five more staples, and we'll head for the coffeepot."

She finished stapling the raccoon — apparently this was part of gluing the hide to the Styrofoam form inside — then led the way over to the house. Once again I found myself on the rustic couch that was covered with knitted afghans. She brought coffee, remembering that I take it black, and I took out a notebook.

"Okay," I said. "How long were you gone yesterday afternoon?"

"An hour, maybe an hour and a half. I went over to Dorinda to the grocery store.

The store there is closer than the Warner Pier Superette. Cheaper, too."

"What time was that?"

"I left about two o'clock."

"So you were back before four?"

"Right."

"Did you lock the house?"

"I doubt it. I don't lock the door very often." She smiled wryly. "Someone might want in."

"Did you notice as soon as you got back that things had been rearranged?"

"No. I put the groceries away; then I went out to the shop and skinned your owl. The museum curator wants it mounted. Flying. It's going to be a nice specimen."

"We'll have to go over and see it. When did you notice things had been moved around?"

"When I came over here from the shop about five o'clock, I looked for the electric bill. I was sure it had been on top of the stack. I finally found it farther down in the pile, under the propane bill."

"Did you see anything else out of place?"

"No. But we're not exactly neat around here. My mother would have said we're not neat at all."

"I'd use the word comfortable. I love your house. How about outside? Was anything moved around out there?"

She shook her head.

"How about in the shop?"

"No, nothing had been disturbed in the shop."

"Do you keep money around?"

"I don't keep cash in either the house or the shop, and I took my purse with me. Most of my customers pay by check. I don't encourage cash. I'm not a good enough bookkeeper to keep good records of cash, and I don't do enough business to justify taking credit cards. Having checks helps me keep track, and that helps when the IRS casts its beady eye on me."

"I expect that Sissy could set you up a simple bookkeeping system."

"Yes, she's offered. But she wants to do it on the computer. I've deliberately avoided any contact with computers. I've even talked Sissy out of having e-mail out here."

"She has Internet access. At least, I found her résumé online."

"She goes to the library if she wants to use the Internet. I don't want Moose Lodge to get that modern. Besides, the only Internet access available out here is the type that uses a regular phone line."

"Dial-up? Yes, there are still big sections of rural Michigan where that's the main thing available."

"Sissy's annoyed with me because I don't even want one of those phones that tells you who's calling."

"Caller ID? That can be pretty convenient."

The contemptuous glance I got from Wildflower scotched that opinion. She spoke again. "Buzz checked his e-mail at the library, too. But I don't think he e-mailed a lot. Chip used to gripe because he had to write him letters. 'Snail mail,' he called it."

"Did the prowler fool with the computer yesterday?"

"You'll have to ask Sissy. But she didn't mention it."

"If the only things disturbed were your desk and Sissy's desk, it looks as if the intruder was looking for some sort of papers. Do you have any idea what those might have been?"

"No. But I have a suspicion of who it was."

"Who?"

"Ace, of course."

"But he's —" I nearly blurted out the first thing that came to mind. Ace Smith had been a high-ranking army officer. It just didn't seem possible that a person who had held a prominent and honored position in society would turn to burglary. However, I had witnessed the threats Ace had made to Sissy, so I paused, then finished my sentence with a new attitude.

"Ace is a complete jerk, isn't he?" I said. "I guess I was thinking of a burglar as a person who sneaks around with a dirty face, wearing raggedy clothes. But I've heard the way Ace Smith can talk. I wouldn't put anything past him."

"I don't know about the way he talks. Usually he's Mr. Cool. I do know that he's wild to get some evidence that will prove Sissy is an unfit mother. I have no doubt that if he found our doors unlocked, he'd just walk in and look around to see what he might find. If he found that Sissy had a Tylenol Three prescription from the dentist — which she doesn't — he'd paint her as a drug addict." She shrugged. "He already thinks I'm a drug addict because I smoked a little pot in my youth. And in Ace's view, I'm un-American because I marched in a few protests."

"I see. I imagine that's a problem with the sheriff, too."

"Right. Burt Ramsey has a very strange idea of what goes on at Moose Lodge. I assure you nothing happens here that's as interesting as the things he imagines."

For the second time I caught a whiff of Wildflower's attitude on the gossip that apparently had swirled around her for years. The first time I met her, she had denied that Moose Lodge had ever harbored nudists. Now she was resentful of how the sheriff regarded her place. She wasn't as indifferent to public opinion as she might pretend to be.

"Okay," I said, "I'll put Ace Smith on my mental list of likely suspects. Your neighbors said you had prowlers around the time Buzz was killed."

"They had prowlers. We never noticed anything over here. Buzz was at home most of the time, you know. It would have been hard to sneak around when he was here."

"That's true. But Nosy and Rosy said they found footprints on their property. Did you find any around here?"

"No. But my drive and parking area are graveled. And it's been dry; there were no traces of mud in the house."

"You say hikers in the nature preserve wander onto your property. I gather you didn't see any yesterday."

"No."

"Nosy and Rosy suspected you'd had a prowler before you did. Why?"

"Because if the prowler approached from

the hiking trail, he'd be likely to cross my property to get to theirs."

"Would you mind if I wandered around for a while? I'd better look at the layout of Moose Lodge."

"That's a good idea."

I put my coffee cup in the kitchen and followed Wildflower out to the back porch. She stood there and pointed out the landmarks visible from the house. The barbed wire fence that divided her property from the Fox Creek Nature Preserve was hidden by trees, but she showed me the path that led to the fence. It was joined by a similar path from the Reagans' property. Inside the preserve, Wildflower said, a footpath ran close to the fence.

"I don't see how people could wander onto your property without guessing that they had left the preserve," I said. "They'd have to climb a barbed wire fence."

Wildflower laughed. "I don't understand it either, but that's what they tell me when I ask them what they're doing here."

I scribbled in my notebook a moment, pretending to make a note. Actually, I was trying to get up the nerve to ask Wildflower a significant question I'd been postponing. I took a deep breath and spoke. "Now, what about Helen Ferguson?"

145

Wildflower's earlier reaction had convinced me that she had run into Helen and that their contact had been important in some way. Was my direct question going to shock her into an answer?

For a moment I thought I'd overstepped. Wildflower didn't blush; she looked angry and spoke in a hard voice. "What makes you think I would know anything about Helen Ferguson?"

"Mainly your reaction when Chip said he didn't know her even as well as you did. You turned bright red."

Another long silence followed. Then Wildflower gave a deep sigh. "Helen and I had a run-in. I don't think Sissy knows about it."

"What happened?"

"Helen came out here snooping. Chip was right when he said she 'nosed around.' She wanted to see Johnny's room, for example. I caught her looking at the electric plugs — as if we wouldn't have baby-proofed them. When I offered her coffee, she followed me into the kitchen and actually opened the cupboards."

Wildflower gave a wicked grin. "Luckily, she didn't find any mice. It was right after Ace filed his custody suit, and Helen was pretty obvious. She was making a scouting trip of some sort."

"I'm surprised you let her in."

"She walked in. I tried to be friendly, but after she used a trip to the potty as an excuse to prowl around in the medicine cabinet, I ordered her out. Told her to skedaddle."

"I don't blame you. Did she go peacefully?"

"Oh yeah. She was trespassing, and she knew it."

After that discussion Wildflower went back to her shop, leaving me to roam around on my own.

As ever, the Moose Lodge terrain scared the heck out of me. I grew up in an area where the main native tree is the mesquite — a short scrubby tree. Oh, there are pecans and oaks and such, but mainly God planned short vegetation for North Texas.

We learned in eighth grade science that if you plant a tree in a forest, it grows tall, trying to reach the light. If you plant the same tree in the open, it grows shorter and broader, because there's light all around it. With plenty of open space, North Texas trees stay short.

Then I moved to Michigan. First of all, our part of Michigan is as flat as Texas ever thought of being, but it's covered with scads of trees — tall trees, growing thickly to-

147

gether. There are bushes and smaller trees in between the tall trees. You can't see the horizon. Lots of times you can't even see the sky.

For a Texas girl, thick forests define the words "irrational fear."

Rationally, I know there's nothing behind those trees. But some primeval fear makes me think there is. I've read that people raised in deep woods find the plains equally frightening because there's nothing to hide behind.

So when I strolled around the Moose Lodge property, I felt pretty antsy. I kept looking all around. So far as I could see, the place was completely deserted, but I was still nervous.

I first circled the two houses, the shop, and another storage building. The second house — the one where Sissy and Buzz had lived — was securely locked. The storage building, a sort of old barn, was unlocked, but it seemed to hold only items that would be useful on a rural property. There was a lawn mower, a rack holding saws and hammers, an old-fashioned scythe, and other old tools. It was even fairly neat, and the floor had recently been swept.

The path Wildflower had pointed out led off to the north. I followed it. Almost immediately, the Moose Lodge buildings disappeared behind the trees and thick undergrowth. I fought my sense of unease and walked on, examining the ground underfoot like an Indian scout.

Who was I kidding? I wouldn't recognize a strange track if I fell in it. I felt extremely inadequate.

I didn't see any footprints, strange or familiar. The path was obviously rarely used. Plants were growing in from the sides, making it narrower and narrower. The path itself was covered with old, sodden leaves. I will say it was quiet. My feet made no noise.

Then I heard voices. I stopped, parted the branches of a bush, and looked ahead.

Hikers. They wore bright T-shirts and carried fanny packs. There were four of them — two adults and two children; a happy family out for a walk. I could even see the fence now. It was between me and the hikers, and it was easy to see because vines were growing over sections of it.

I stopped until the hikers went by. They made no move toward climbing over the fence, and they didn't seem to notice I was there.

As soon as they disappeared to my right, I went on to the fence. I thought I'd walked about a quarter of a mile away from the

Moose Lodge buildings.

The fence was strongly built. It was barbed wire and had four strands. It didn't look as if it would be easy to get over, but as a Texas girl I'd climbed enough pasture fences — constructed of what Texans pronounce "bob war" — to know how to do it. You hang on to a post and step on the wire near where it's attached to the post. You go up like a ladder and step over carefully, placing your shoe sole between the barbs. I could have climbed that fence easily, though I might have had to follow up with a tetanus shot.

I looked at the ground near the fence. There were still no tracks in the path, and there were no shreds of tobacco, billfolds containing ID cards, earrings, scraps of fabric caught on a barb, or other clues usually left behind by villains in mystery novels.

I stood still and looked up and down the fence line. I was completely alone. Yes, someone could have climbed over and followed the path to Wildflower's house. But there was nothing to show that someone had.

I spoke aloud. "Lee, you're an idiot. Just because you were mad at the sheriff, you said you'd try to help Wildflower. But there's not a darn thing you can do."

At that moment I felt a vibration in my

hip pocket and heard a noise like an old-fashioned telephone. My cell phone was ringing.

I was almost surprised that Moose Lodge had service. There are big areas around the lakeshore that don't. Inland, coverage improves.

I answered. "Lee Woodyard."

"It's Aunt Nettie. A couple of things happened I thought you might want to know about."

"What now?"

"Hogan came by. First, the medical examiner called with his report."

"On Helen Ferguson?"

"Right. Hogan says — well, it looks as if somebody hit her in the back of the neck with something. And it probably happened about an hour before she fell down the stairs at the beach. They don't think the injury is consistent with falling, at least not where she was found."

"She was murdered?"

"Killed, anyway. You know how Hogan is about using the word 'murder' when it might be manslaughter."

"I guess I'm not too surprised. What was the other thing that happened?"

"It was later. I wasn't here. Three different ladies have told me the story, so I'm not

151

sure I understand."

"What, Aunt Nettie? What happened?"

"One of the state police detectives said they had to talk to Sissy again. He took her down to the police station."

CHAPTER 12

If I got to the Warner Pier Police Department in one piece, it was because I can drive with my subconscious in charge. I have no memory of running back to my van, or tearing out Wildflower's drive, or of the fifteen miles to Warner Pier. I returned to consciousness only as I squealed to an illegal stop in a handicapped slot — the only one open — outside the combination city hall and police station in the center of town.

I ran into the station, passed Hogan's secretary without so much as a nod, and burst through the little swinging gate that tells visitors to stop. It didn't tell *me* to stop. I kicked that sucker open without hesitating.

And there, with her green eyes wide open in surprise at my precipitous arrival, was Sissy.

She was sitting in an upright chair outside Hogan's office. Her purse was in her lap, and she had her hands neatly folded.

"Lee?" Her tone was incredulous. "Is something wrong?"

Luckily there was a chair beside her. I fell into it. "Maybe not," I said. "What are you doing here?"

"The state police asked me to make a formal statement about what happened last night."

I'd gotten all excited about a routine law-enforcement procedure. I began to laugh.

"Why are you here?" Sissy said.

"Gossip again. Aunt Nettie got a third-hand story about your being asked to come down to the police station, and she panicked. Or I panicked."

"I'm just waiting for the statement to be typed up so I can sign it." Sissy grinned her impish grin. "I'm glad somebody gives a darn."

I should have remembered she had to make a statement about finding Helen's body. Joe might have to make one, too.

I took a deep breath, feeling like a fool. "I can't influence what happens to you, but I can make sure someone calls a lawyer."

Before I could say anything else, the door to Hogan's office opened, and there was a bubble of conversation as three men came out.

"I naturally want to see this cleared up fast," a deep voice said. "For someone who worked for me to be killed — well, if nothing else, it's embarrassing."

Embarrassing? That was a peculiar adjective to apply to a violent death. Who was with Hogan?

I turned my head and saw Ace Smith.

I quickly looked back at Sissy. She nodded to Ace coolly, and Ace stepped toward her as if he was going to speak.

But Hogan intervened. "Sissy," he said, "you're next. I'd like to go over your statement with you before you go."

"Certainly." Sissy stood up and went into Hogan's office without flicking an eyelash toward her father-in-law.

Hogan turned toward Ace. "Your statement will be typed up in a few minutes, Colonel Smith."

"Please call me Ace."

"Sure. Would you mind waiting until the statement is ready? Then we won't have to track you down to get it signed."

Ace nodded, and Hogan turned toward his office. But Ace tapped his arm and led him away from the door. This meant they were standing close to me. Ace spoke in a low voice. "Chief Jones, I know you're aware of the way people can dodge questions."

"I'd better be."

Ace shuffled his feet and looked around the office. Why was he looking so ill at ease? I opened my purse and began to dig around in it, giving what I hoped was an imitation of a woman totally concentrating on her own affairs. In a moment Ace spoke again, this time barely above a whisper, but I could hear him.

"Chief Jones, some law-enforcement officers have underestimated how slick Sissy is."

Hogan didn't say anything.

Ace went on. "She's . . . well, insidious. Tricky. She has this innocent act that can be very misleading."

"I'll be very careful as I question her, Colonel Smith."

"I'm sure you will." Ace leaned even closer to Hogan, and his whisper took on an anguished tone. "I found out about her the hard way. She took my son away from me. And then she killed him."

He turned away, blinking. He sat down across from me, put his elbows on his knees, and stared at the floor. Only a monster wouldn't have felt sorry for him.

For the first time I believed that Ace Smith actually thought Sissy had killed Buzz. In his eyes she was the person who pulled the trigger. Her alibi, proving she was thirty miles away, meant nothing to him. I understood why he was trying to gain custody of Johnny. No wonder he had lit into Sissy in the grocery store.

Until that moment I hadn't analyzed why Ace was so down on Sissy. I guess I had thought it was something simple, such as he didn't approve of her hippie grandmother or he thought Buzz could have married someone from a more socially prominent family. No, the real reason was much more serious.

I was concentrating so hard as I took all this in that I jumped when someone said my name.

"Lee?" It was Hogan. "Did you need something?"

"No. No, I just had a question for Sissy. I'm leaving now. I'll be off about my own burglary. I mean, business! My own business."

Oh ye gods! My twisted tongue had told the world what I was up to. I might as well have announced I was looking into the burglary at Moose Lodge. I hoped I didn't seem as confused as I felt as I jumped up and ran for the door.

Outside, I stopped. Where was I going? I'd told Aunt Nettie I was taking the after-

157

noon off, so I didn't need to go to the office. Did I want to return to Moose Lodge and hunt burglars some more? Or was there something else I should be doing?

At any rate, I needed to move my van out of the handicapped slot, the one such spot in a row of eight parking spaces outside city hall. Being the niece by marriage of the police chief wasn't going to save me from a major fine if Hogan's patrolman came by and caught me.

I moved toward the row of cars, but a voice stopped me. "Lee? Did you have to make a statement, too?"

I turned and found myself facing Chip.

"So far they haven't asked for one. I'd be one of the minor witnesses, since I never went down to the beach. I guess you had to make one."

"I will have to, as you said. But I don't know anything."

"Colonel Smith is in there now."

"I don't think he knows anything either. He went into Holland for dinner with some people last night. He didn't get back until after Helen's body had been found."

"An alibi. Lucky guy."

I glanced at my watch even though I didn't have to be anywhere. "I guess I'd better be on my way."

Chip nodded. He turned toward the police station, and I moved toward my van. But before Chip could reach the door, Ace Smith came out it. To my surprise, he brushed by Chip and came toward me.

"Young woman, are you Lee Woodyard?"

"Yes."

"You're the person who gave Sissy a job."

"My aunt and I hired her at TenHuis Chocolade."

He gave me a big friendly smile, but his next remark was not so friendly. "I feel I should warn you that Sissy's not honest."

Hmmm. I didn't know what to say to that one. Ask him to prove it? Or would that just start a big discussion I didn't want to get into?

But I had to reply. "Don't worry, Colonel Smith. We have plenty of accounting safeguards in place."

"Oh, I don't mean she'd steal. Not money."

I gave him my own big friendly smile. "We also have limits on how much chocolate employees are permitted to eat."

His reply was a look of deep sadness. "I see you're not taking me seriously, Mrs. Woodyard."

He was apparently determined to go into the matter of Sissy's employment and her

159

character right there on the street. I could feel my temper rising, and I had a strong desire to tell him to butt out. I looked around. Luckily not too many tourists hang out around the police station, but we weren't completely alone. Several groups of people were walking along the sidewalk. But even if we had been alone, the last thing I wanted was a slanging match with a man I'd never even spoken to before in my life.

So I kept smiling. "I don't think we need to discuss this," I said. I turned toward the van.

Ace barked out a laugh. "I see you're a fitting pal for Sissy. A rule breaker. Another conniver."

He was obviously trying to goad me into making an unwise remark. He was speaking loudly and drawing attention from the others on the street. I wondered if he had selected a public street for this conversation to add to the gossip about Sissy — and to add me to it.

So I didn't say anything.

But Ace kept talking. "You're proving that my opinion is right. See, you've taken a handicapped parking space. One you have no right to!"

At that, I did turn around and speak. I guess he expected me to act embarrassed.

160

But I had a different question. I kept my voice quiet as I asked it.

"How did you know which vehicle is mine?"

I'd struck home. I was surprised at the shocked look that came over Ace's face.

I followed up. "I usually park in back of the shop this time of the year. Have you been trolling our alley? Or did you see the van at my house? Were you out there last night when Helen Ferguson fell down the steps at the beach?"

Colonel Ace Smith turned bright red and walked away, headed back into the police station. I realized Chip was standing twenty feet down the curb. He grinned at me, but he didn't speak. And he didn't follow Ace inside the station.

I was finally able to get into the van, but, as the motor turned over, I saw Hogan in front of the police station. He was waving at me.

I rolled the window down and called to him. "I'm moving it!"

Hogan grinned. He walked up to the van, holding a brown paper sack. When he spoke, he used his usual booming bass voice. "I know you don't usually nab a handicapped slot, Lee. And it's not Ace Smith's responsibility to enforce our parking laws around here."

"You heard all that?"

"Oh, yeah."

"I'm serious about wanting to know how he recognized my van."

"I'll ask him. But you do still have that Dallas Cowboys sticker in the back window."

"But how would he know I'm from Texas?"

"You're notorious." Hogan shoved his paper sack toward me.

"What's this?"

"It's casting material. I thought you might want to cast a few footprints."

My jaw nearly hit the steering wheel. Was Hogan telling me he knew I was investigating the burglary? And was he telling me it was all right with him?

He leaned in the window, and his face grew serious. "Be careful," he said. "Somebody's playing rough."

CHAPTER 13

At least Hogan had made my mind up for me.

I ran by TenHuis Chocolade and scooped an old beat-up metal mixing bowl out of the storage room, several plastic spoons out of the break room, and a couple of bottles of water from the refrigerator. Then I headed east out of Warner Pier. Nosy and Rosy said they had found footprints, and Hogan apparently thought it would be a good thing to have a cast of them.

Not that the cast, made by an amateur detective, would be very good evidence. But even if it wasn't an official clue, it might give some real investigator a hint.

Luckily, Joe and I had taken a course for citizens who were interested in becoming police department volunteers, so I had an elementary idea of how to use the dental compound today's law officers use for casting. Now I just hoped Nosy and Rosy were home. I didn't want to go onto their property without permission. That would probably bring another report of prowlers.

The next mailbox east of Moose Lodge was marked with the name Reagan. It was shaped like a great big fish; the postman poked the mail in through a wide-open mouth. At the end of the drive I saw a small black pickup truck. Good. Maybe Nosy and Rosy were there.

The Reagans' property wasn't as neatly kept as Wildflower's. The woods were thick over almost all of it, with only a small patch cleared for a scraggly bit of grass and one flower bed. In the little clearing was a light gray double-wide with a colonial-style front porch. The double-wide would have made me feel as if I were back in Texas if it hadn't been for the tall trees and thick undergrowth.

Actually, the undergrowth was much too thick to suit me. The whole property felt damp and claustrophobic. I gave a shiver as I stopped the van, and I couldn't have guessed if that shiver was caused by the clammy atmosphere or by the threatening vibes I was picking up from all those trees.

It was the kind of area I call "mosquito heaven," and I was glad to see that hanging on the porch was a big bug light, the kind that attracts bugs, then electrocutes them.

As I got out of the van, Rosy came out the front door. His white hair was fluffed up in back, and I wondered if he'd been taking a nap when he heard my van.

He looked a little puzzled; then his face cleared. "Mrs. Woodyard, right? What can we do for you?"

"Wildflower wasn't happy with the cursory way the sheriff was investigating the possible burglary at her house. She asked me to look around and see if I could find any more evidence that someone had been prowling around. And you folks said that y'all found some tracks."

"Darn right! And that sheriff wouldn't even look at them. I guess we're not important enough in the Warner County picture for him to pay us any mind."

"Would you mind if I took a look?"

"Not at all! I'll show you where they are."

"Did the prowler get into your house?"

"I didn't find any sign of that. We lock up pretty good. We lived in the big city too long to have this small-town habit of leaving things open the way Wildflower does."

Rosy led around the house, and I followed, bringing the casting materials. "Then you haven't lived here too long?" I said.

"Just about five years. We were looking for

a cheap place to retire."

"Do you find it lonely?"

"After thirty years in an apartment complex, we like lonely. And Wildflower is a good neighbor."

Rosy led the way down an extension of the gravel drive. We walked around another group of trees and reached a metal outbuilding. A double garage door was centered in front of the drive, and an ordinary outside door was around the corner, on the side of the building. True to what Rosy had said, both doors were firmly closed and had locks.

An old-fashioned galvanized steel washtub had been turned upside down at the corner of the building. Rosy lifted the tub and made a dramatic gesture. "There!"

The tub had been protecting the suspicious tracks. Someone had definitely been walking in the damp earth around the Reagans' garage.

At first I could see only the outline of a shoe sole in one place. Then I saw others that were not so clear. When I peered closely at them, the tracks looked as if someone had been stomping on waffles. The clearest print showed a pattern of diamonds running down the center of the sole and some wavy lines toward the toe.

And the prints looked big. I belatedly realized I hadn't brought a measuring tape.

I got out my notebook, knelt down, and made a sketch of the clearest print on a fresh page. I drew the pattern in, and I gauged the size by comparing it with my hand.

Rosy watched me. "Do you want to measure it?"

"Do you have a ruler I could use?"

"Sure. There's a measuring tape right here in the workshop."

Rosy went to a side door of the metal building, took a key from somewhere behind a bush, and unlocked the door. So much for keeping everything locked up. I hid a grin, but I didn't criticize his security procedures aloud.

In a minute Rosy came back with a tape measure, a stout metal one with a button to retract the measuring tape.

The print in the mud had been made by a shoe or boot thirteen inches long. It was five inches wide at the widest point, across the ball of the foot. I marked that down. Then I produced my pan, spoons, and water and began to mix the dental compound. It should be the consistency of pancake batter, Hogan had told our class. Investigators use it because it sets much faster than plaster of Paris.

Rosy sighed. "I wish I'd known how to do that last February, when I found the tracks before Buzz was killed."

"Did they look like these?"

"Not much. It was winter, after all. Whoever came in had on some sort of snow boots. But if I'd thought to measure them, at least, it might have helped. Of course, we didn't know somebody was going to get killed." He moved restlessly. "Now — well, I can't help wondering if the person who prowled around last winter is the same one who's been here in the past couple of days."

Rosy watched for another moment, then glanced at his wrist. "Do you mind if I leave you with this project?"

"Not at all. Would it be okay if I looked around a few more places?"

"Sure! That's fine. I've just got a chore I need to do."

At that moment I heard Nosy's voice, calling from the house, over behind the trees. "Rosy! It's time for *Jeopardy!*"

So much for Rosy's claim he was going to do chores; I was interrupting an afternoon-television ritual. Rosy told me he'd leave the workshop door open and that I could put the measuring tape on the workbench. Then he left me alone. This was good, because I'm a total amateur at casting a

168

footprint, and I'd just as soon not have a witness to my inept way of doing it.

Hogan might have laughed at the way I cast the print, but I got it done, by golly. Then I cast a couple of the other, more smudged tracks. The material set quickly, so pretty soon I was able to stack the casts on the gravel drive. Then I looked around to see if the prowler had left any other signs.

And farther from the metal building I found another print of a different shoe. This one was of a smooth-soled shoe.

It took me a minute to see that the print must have been made by Rosy. At least, there were two of them, side by side, right where he'd been standing as he watched me prepare to make the mold of the waffle-soled boot.

Rosy's tracks looked to be the same size as the ones with the waffle soles.

I studied them, comparing them. Co-incidence, I told myself. In fact, I doubted it was true.

I knelt and measured Rosy's print. It was thirteen inches long and five inches wide across the ball of the foot. The two prints were the same length.

Did this mean the intruder's foot was the same size as Rosy's? Were they the same height? Or were the feet inside the shoes smaller? Did Rosy own a pair of hiking boots? Had he made the suspect tracks himself? If so, why would he tell Wildflower and the sheriff and everybody else that they were made by some stranger?

It would take a real expert to confirm that both tracks might have been made by the same person wearing different shoes.

I reminded myself that Rosy had told me I could look around their property. Was I going to get that done or just stand around gawking at the ground?

I carefully stacked the casts and my materials — bowl, spoons, casting compound — on the gravel drive. I put the measuring tape inside the workshop. Then I walked around the metal building.

A couple of paths led away from Rosy's workshop, going into the woods. I followed one of them. It went about forty feet and ended in a trash heap, a pile of stuff that in a rural area has to be hauled to the dump by the property owner. A rusty metal bookshelf too big for regular trash pickup leaned against a broken metal chair. I retraced my steps and followed another path. It led to a pit Nosy and Rosy apparently used as a compost heap. I backed away from it gingerly; I was sure raccoons and skunks and other critters hung out there, even though dirt had been tossed on top of the garbage.

A third path led in a northerly direction and I went on farther, ignoring my usual fears. Eventually I came to the fence that bordered the nature preserve. I realized I'd crossed over onto Wildflower's property.

All was peaceful there. The day Joe and I had hiked the nature preserve, somebody had been riding an all-terrain vehicle along the trails, even though use of such things was illegal. But now it was quiet.

I examined the fence and saw no sign that anyone had climbed it. I scanned the woods on the nature preserve side. They were just as thick and brushy as the ones on Nosy and Rosy's and on Wildflower's property. A faint path led into them.

I had no desire to go in there. I looked at the underbrush, gave another little shudder, and turned back, retracing my steps along the path until I saw the metal building. Having no idea what I was looking for, I was unlikely to find it. I'd done enough, I decided. I'd gather up my materials and go home.

As I came around the corner of the building, I saw that my stuff had been disturbed. The plastic sack I'd used to carry the dental compound, the metal bowl, and the water bottles had been turned over, its contents scattered over the gravel.

My first thought was that an animal had been there.

But why would the sack have attracted an animal? There was nothing edible in it.

Then I got close enough to see the casts I had made. They were smashed to pieces.

"Oh no!" I yelped out the words.

Well, that eliminated animals. No animal would have broken up the casts. Someone had kicked or stomped on them or hit them with a club.

I stomped my own foot. "Son of a gun! Drat!" I said. Or something like that.

"Well, by golly, I'll just make another set," I said.

I turned to the corner of the workshop, where the tub had protected the tracks.

The tub had been tossed aside, and the area it had hidden had been raked thoroughly.

The tracks were gone.

I could have cried. The evidence had been destroyed.

I didn't know if I should cry or swear. As I was trying to decide, I heard a noise.

It was a branch breaking, and it came from the direction of the nature preserve.

I have never understood what possessed me, but I turned and ran toward the sound.

CHAPTER 14

Why did I do that? Looking back, I'm not sure.

Maybe I ran toward the strange sound simply out of anger. I'd worked hard making molds of those tracks. It hadn't taken a lot of physical labor, true, but it had taken mental effort because it wasn't a job I was familiar with. I had done something I wasn't at all sure I could do, something I'd had only rudimentary lessons in accomplishing. And I'd succeeded. To see my work destroyed — well, it made me mad as all get-out.

So I ran down that path, ready to tear into whoever had ruined the tracks and the molds I had made.

I was so mad that I'd gone at least a hundred yards before I realized I was running headlong into a situation I dreaded and always tried to avoid. It took me that long to come to myself and realize I was surrounded by deep woods and there was someone dangerous near.

Cold fingers slid down my spine. My running steps slowed to a walk. Then my walk slowed to a sort of tiptoe; I edged along, trying to look in every direction at once — at the trees, through the trees, behind the trees.

After all, you never can tell when something scary is going to jump out from behind a tree. Trees are like that. They hide things — animals, dangerous maniacs, monsters, snakes, poison ivy, crawly insects, small dinosaurs, nameless fears, even harmless little creatures like squirrels that could startle you.

But most of all, trees hide the sky. They make you feel closed in and claustrophobic. They make it hard to breathe.

One tree is a friend, providing shade and beauty. A thousand trees are a net of spiderwebs, every branch grabbing and trying to catch you, or camouflaging unknown enemies.

I shuddered and stopped in my tracks. I almost turned and went back.

But ahead I could see the fence that marked the boundary of the nature preserve. At least I could go that far. I might still be able to get a look at the person who had smashed the molds and destroyed the foot-prints.

So I walked on. I tried to step out firmly, but I didn't run. In fact, it would have been hard to run on that path. It wasn't a main-tained path, but merely a partly overgrown trail, narrow and covered with leaf mold and scattered branches and twigs.

Forcing myself to be brave helped, of course. When I came to the fence, I paused and looked ahead. I saw nothing significant. Nobody yelled boo. Nobody jumped out with a club. No wild animal howled.

I decided I could check on what was on the other side of the boundary. I climbed up, using the barbed wire like a ladder and holding on to the nearest fence post, then jumped down on the other side. The path continued, still faint and hard to see. I walked along, watching my footing. After all, rationally I knew that the worst danger in a forest is the chance of tripping and breaking a leg. If I got stranded in the nature preserve, it might be a long time before someone found me. So I pussy-footed along, stepping carefully and remind-ing myself that my cell phone was in my pocket. Of course, it might not have any service in an area this remote.

After another twenty-five yards I came to

a wider path, the walking trail that circled the entire nature preserve. I felt as if I had reached civilization. Here was a trail that showed signs of attention. Logs were laid along the sides to delineate its borders. The occasional small stump showed that it had been deliberately cleared for the use of hikers.

Silence hung heavy. I didn't hear footsteps or twigs breaking or anything else that indicated I wasn't alone. No hikers appeared. There was no sign of anybody else anywhere. I stared up and down the new trail. There wasn't anybody. The person who had destroyed the tracks seemed to have escaped. I decided I might as well go back.

I turned around, and between the fence and me a bush moved.

Immediately I knew the person I had chased was still there.

If a whole lot of trees and bushes move in a forest, it means the wind is blowing. But if only one moves, that's a different matter. Something moved that bush, and it wasn't the wind. The wind wouldn't move only one thing at a time. Some living creature made that bush move.

That was the moment I realized what a bad position I'd placed myself in. I had begun the chase simply hoping to see who had destroyed the tracks. I wanted to give that person a piece of my mind. If I'd come up behind him on the trail, I would have scolded him. I had been so mad I hadn't stopped to realize that my chasing him might make him feel very threatened.

Now, belatedly, I realized I was in an awkward, even dangerous, position. After all, there had been a murder near this place four months earlier. I didn't expect the killer to still be hanging around, but bad things had happened near there, and I'd been foolish to forget it. I shouldn't have come, and I ought to have turned back.

But that suspicious bush was between me and the fence. I decided I wasn't going back down the path that led to the Reagans' house. Even if I made it to the fence without getting ambushed, I'd be in an extremely vulnerable position as I climbed over, using barbed wire as a ladder.

So how was I going to get out of there? I turned back to the public path. When Joe and I had hiked it a couple of months previous, in early spring, the undergrowth hadn't been nearly as thick, and I hadn't been alone, so my tree phobia hadn't bothered me. Now I was going to have to tackle it on my own. At least I wasn't completely unfamiliar with the area.

The main path circled the boundaries of the nature preserve, following a four-mile route, according to the signpost I remembered at the main entrance. But other paths crisscrossed through the center of the area.

I turned left, west. I wasn't sure of exactly where I was, but I thought that would be the shortest route to the entrance. I certainly didn't want to walk three or four miles going the long way round, and I was afraid to tackle the paths that cut across the middle; I'd get lost in a minute.

I walked rapidly, but I didn't run. Running could lead to falling, and if the guy behind the bush — I decided it was a man — came after me, he might catch up while I was trying to get back on my feet. There was also that broken-leg scenario to consider. So I walked fast, but I didn't run.

When I saw a dead branch on the ground, I picked it up. It was too long and heavy to lug along. By cracking it against a tree and stepping on the shattered end, I was able to break it off into a club about the size and weight of a baseball bat. It wasn't much, but having it made me feel better.

The trail was open and level, neatly maintained by the nature preserve staff, so I moved right along. But now and then I looked back to see if anyone was coming after me.

I never saw anything but trees. That was the good news and the bad news.

I never saw a giant wolf, slobbering and ready to tear my throat out. I never saw a maniac, rolling his eyes madly.

But trees could be hiding anything and anybody. Trees made everything dark and gloomy. Trees hid the horizon. Trees kept me from taking a deep breath.

I reminded myself that I came from pioneer stock on both the Michigan and Texas sides. I was tough. I was certainly not going to be sent into a panic by an object rooted to the ground, an object that couldn't chase me or even throw pinecones.

I kept walking as rapidly as possible, and I kept looking back down the path. Once I came to a straight stretch of trail that extended several hundred yards. For that piece of trail, I ran. Then I jumped behind a cedar tree and peeked through its branches, looking back to see if any follower came out behind me.

None did. But I would have sworn something back there had moved.

Or maybe I couldn't swear to it. I thought the undergrowth shook, but no figure appeared on the path.

After two or three minutes, I decided there

were three explanations. First, the follower wasn't very close. Second, he didn't want to catch up with me. Third, the whole thing was my imagination. I ran for another hundred yards, then returned to my quick walk.

I tried to reassure myself. I thought of the moving bush, the one that had sent me on this excursion. I told myself that if the person who destroyed the tracks had been hiding behind the bush, he didn't seem to mean me any harm. He could have attacked me as I climbed the fence to get into the preserve. I'd been in an extremely vulnerable position at that moment, and nothing had happened.

Pooh, pooh, I told myself. You've over-reacted completely. The guy may have wanted to destroy evidence, but he obviously didn't want to hurt you.

I was feeling so confident that I didn't even hesitate when I came to a fork in the path. I simply remembered the map board at the entrance to the nature preserve. Staying on the perimeter trail required always taking the left-hand path. Ignoring the path that probably cut across the middle of the preserve, I went on.

I had walked quite a way by then. Surely the entrance to the nature preserve wasn't too much farther. I'd passed a lot of the educational signboards that explained what was in the preserve. Look at the beaver dam, look at the beech trees, look at the irises that marked where a pioneer cabin had stood. I began to feel confident that I'd be out of there shortly.

Then what was I going to do? Walk back down the gravel road to the Reagans' house, where my car was? Call Joe and ask him for a ride? Call Wildflower and ask her to pick me up? I certainly wasn't going to hitch-hike.

I was thinking ahead, about how to get home, when the trail made a hard right.

And a tree ran out and attacked me.

Now, I'm not saying I fell over a tree or ran into a tree or tripped on the root of a tree. I mean that a cedar tree about six feet tall came out of a side path on my right and ran at me.

It was growling. I jumped backward and gave a shriek that would have passed for the rebel yell passed down in my dad's family.

The tree kept coming. I swung my club and gave it a pretty good rap on its left side. That didn't bother the tree. One of its branches whacked me in the face, and another shoved at my midsection, knocking the wind out of me. I fell back — I believe it's known as "ass over teakettle" — and landed on my back in a large bush of some kind. Then the tree ran down the path to my right.

It left me stuck in the bush, gasping for air. It must have been a full minute before I rolled out of the prickly shrub and found myself on my hands and knees on the path. Even then all I could do was try to breathe. After several more minutes of gasping, I began to catch my breath. Then I began to analyze what had happened.

First, my club had been of little use. I'd been so startled by the idea of an attacking tree that I had managed only one blow, and that one hadn't seemed to bother the tree.

Second, what had seemed to be a tree had actually been a person holding a large branch. A stray limb might have hit me in the face, but those hadn't been twigs that punched me in the stomach. That had been somebody's fist.

Third, I couldn't possibly describe the tree-person. He'd seemed tall, but a branch might have been sticking up higher than his head. He'd looked green, but that was cloth-ing. Could he have been wearing camou-flage? Or the forest green–patterned cloth-ing popular with hikers and bird-watchers? His face had been hidden by the tree branches he carried, but from the few glimpses I could see showing through, it had also been a strange color of brown — not a human color. I decided the tree-man had painted his face. Maybe he had covered it with dirt.

Fourth, the tree-man seemed to know where the paths led. He must be familiar with the preserve. He had cut across the middle of the preserve and cut me off.

Fifth, I had to get out of there.

I got to my feet, picked up my club — it might be some protection sometime — and started walking rapidly. I had to get back to civilization.

I had walked less than five minutes when I heard voices. This was not, at first, reassuring. After all, rotten guys can talk. But I kept going, and I saw yellow spots through the trees. I turned around a curve and saw a group of around twenty little boys, all in yellow T-shirts and khaki shorts.

Campers. The nature preserve was used by all sorts of youth and children's groups, of course. These little guys were accompanied by three big strong masculine adults wearing yellow shirts marked COUNSELOR. They looked incredibly handsome. I was willing to bet those three guys could fight off a tree without turning a hair.

I walked up to them and joined their group. I held my club behind me, hoping I didn't look threatening. And I realized I had been right about being close to the nature preserve's entrance. The boys and their counselors were clumped around the first educational exhibit on the trail, the one that explained the history of the preserve.

The tallest counselor was expounding on the exhibit.

"The first Horace T. Fox cut down trees," the counselor said. "You may have already learned that Michigan was practically stripped of its trees early in its history. The pioneers came in, cut the trees, built saw-mills, and shipped lumber on the Great Lakes. America was building towns and cit-ies, so lots of lumber was needed. The entire state of Michigan was stripped of its trees."

The counselors and the boys were eyeing me, obviously curious as to why a giant blond woman, panting slightly and holding a club, had suddenly joined their group, but I smiled, and no one asked me what the heck I was doing.

"Today, areas like this one are called 'second growth.' The trees here grew up to replace the trees the pioneers cut down. But the great-grandson of Horace T. Fox saw that forests should be preserved, as well as cut down and used to build houses and stores. So he gave this preserve — thousands of acres of trees — to the public so that people can enjoy forests."

Then a sound came from the parking lot. Someone gunned a motor.

"Oh no!" I said aloud and vigorously.

I ran to the short path leading to the entrance, turned hard, and rushed into the parking lot.

An absolutely ordinary gray sedan was digging out of the lot. It threw gravel as it turned onto the road. And then it was gone.

I didn't see it well enough to guess the make or see the license plate or get a peek at the driver.

Had it been my pursuer?

Chocolate Chat

In her book *The Healing Powers of Chocolate,* author Cal Orey devotes a chapter to home remedies involving chocolate. Here are some of her suggestions.

Anxiety — Although chocolate contains small amounts of caffeine and some sugar, it's still soothing to the emotions. She suggests a half ounce of premium dark chocolate and a glass of water before an event you feel may cause anxiety.

Bone Loss — A daily serving of chocolate milk or hot chocolate will add milk to your diet, and milk contains magnesium, manganese, and calcium for bone health.

Digestive Problems — Try chocolate with peppermint.

Hot Flashes — Try a cold chocolate drink, or have a couple of truffles that contain green tea.

Seasonal Affective Disorder (SAD) — Hot cocoa to the rescue. Use cocoa with a high cocoa content, but cut calories by using one or two percent milk.

CHAPTER 15

"Can I help you?"

I jumped all over and whirled around when I heard the voice behind me, but it was only one of the yellow-shirted counselors. He looked to be about twenty, a big ugly guy with a crew cut and muscles. I toyed with the idea of telling him the whole story. Then I toyed with making up a lie — "I had a fight with my boyfriend, and he's driven off and left me."

I finally went with an abbreviated version of the truth. I told him I believed someone had been stalking me through the preserve. I had hoped to get a look at him, I said. Now I thought he had cut through the woods, gotten into his car, and driven off before I could see who it was.

"You probably think I'm one of those women who belittles — I mean, believes! I sound like one of those women who has the idea men are after her all the time," I said.

"I don't *think* I am."

He smiled. "Is your car here?"

"No. I was visiting friends whose property adjoins the preserve, and I entered from the south side. My car's over there."

"Would a ride back help?"

I sighed with relief. "It would be a lifesaver. Of course, your only alternative is allowing a strange and possibly deranged woman to join the campers on their nature walk. I do not want to go back the whole way alone."

"Let me tell the other counselors where I'm going."

My new pal's name was Dick. I held on to my club as he gave me a lift back to the Reagans' drive in the camp's van. I told him to come by TenHuis Chocolade for a free box of chocolates. We parted happily.

I said good-bye to the Reagans, and I almost left without telling them about the disaster that had happened to the tracks. I decided I had to, however. If someone was still prowling around their property, they had a right to know.

Rosy replied by showing me a little plaque outside their front door. THESE PREMISES GUARDED BY SMITH & WESSON.

"I'll remember that," I said. "If I have to come back, I'll call first." He chortled happily. He certainly didn't seem nervous about the prowler. That was interesting. After all, there had been a murder practically next door.

I went back to Rosy's workshop to make sure I'd replaced his tools properly. As I was putting the rake in the corner, I felt something in my pocket. It was my notebook.

Aha! At least I had a sketch of the mysterious footprints. It showed the pattern on the sole of the prowler's shoe, and it was marked with the dimensions of the tracks.

"At least it's something," I said aloud.

I drove back to Warner Pier and went straight to the police department. At this point it was nearly five o'clock, but obviously Hogan, with a suspicious death to investigate, wouldn't be taking off early — or maybe at all. I planned to wait until he could see me so I could tell him about the big chase in the nature preserve.

But Hogan, his one-woman office staff said, was out and hadn't indicated when he'd be back.

"I hope he's eating dinner," she said. "He never stopped for lunch. Of course, you're welcome to wait. But I don't see any point in it. I'll page him and tell him you came by."

Finding Hogan and telling him about the

chase was obviously a dim hope. I went to my office and wrote an account of the chase and the damage to the footprints and the casts I'd made, as well as the damage to my rib cage and the twigs in my hair. I printed it out and gave it to Aunt Nettie. I told her to pin it to Hogan's pillow or put it in his breakfast cereal so he could look at it at his convenience.

Then I went home, made a gin and tonic for me, and opened a beer for Joe — just one each. He didn't know it yet, but he was taking me out for dinner even if it was just pizza at the Dock Street.

He didn't object to my plan, and he listened while I described my afternoon. He didn't even tell me I'd been stupid to chase the guy into the forest preserve. I'd figured that out for myself. He did make a couple of remarks about Hogan's encouraging me to go out there.

"That was police business," he said. "If Hogan thought it should be done, he should have gone out there himself."

"He couldn't, Joe. He and the sheriff are already at odds, and the Reagans' house is way outside Hogan's jurisdiction."

Joe gave a derisive laugh. "Hogan knows enough people in the state police to get things done. He shouldn't have put you in danger."

"Maybe the whole thing was my imagination."

"Breaking up the casts and destroying the original footprints? And knocking you into a bush? It's hard to say that was your imagination."

"I have a feeling Sheriff Ramsey could say it was. Or he'd say I lied." I finished my drink and stood up. "Let's go eat."

We were just opening the door when the phone rang. It was Hogan.

"Okay," he said. "Who did you tell before you went out there to cast those footprints?"

I stood there feeling like an idiot.

Of course. Someone had to know I was interested in the footprints, or that person wouldn't have gone out to the Reagans' place to destroy them. I should have realized that.

"Duh! I can't believe I didn't think about that."

"Think about it now. Did you tell Nettie? Sissy? Joe?"

"No. I didn't tell any of them. I didn't tell a soul."

"Nettie already said you didn't tell her, but you must have told someone."

"No. After you gave me the casting material, I ran by the office and got an old mix-

191

ing bowl, a plastic spoon, and some bottled water. I didn't tell anybody why I needed it. I just told Aunt Nettie I was going to take the rest of the afternoon off. I made sure Sissy had work to do, but I didn't tell her where I was going. I just went."

"Did you call anyone?"

"No."

"Text anyone?"

"No. I just drove out there." I gasped. "Wait a minute! How about the Reagans? They knew what I was doing."

"We'll have to ask them if they told anyone."

"They mainly seemed to be concerned with watching *Jeopardy!* If either of them went anywhere, they didn't take the pickup that was sitting there. Wait another minute! Ace Smith! He had just walked off when you came out to talk to me. Could he have overheard us?"

"Colonel Ace Smith did not go out there." Hogan chuckled. "He was tied up at my office all afternoon, and he has the high blood pressure to prove it."

I couldn't help laughing. "I guess people around here are just not as respectful of the colonel as he might wish."

"We're as respectful as he deserves. I'm a little tired of being ordered around as if I'm a PFC."

Hogan asked me a few more questions designed to figure out who might have known I was going to the Reagans' to look at footprints. Had I stopped for gasoline? Had I asked directions? Had I seen anyone I knew as I drove out there? The answer to each of the questions was no.

But his comments, particularly about Colonel Smith, had aroused my curiosity. After Joe and I got back from dinner, I went to the computer in the corner of the bedroom, went online, and prepared to search for Colonel Ace Smith. And while I was at it, I decided I might as well take a look at the history of Nosy and Rosy Reagan. In fact, I decided to start with them. After all, it wasn't going to be hard to track down a man named Roosevelt Reagan who had lived in Detroit.

Sure enough, the Web page of a Detroit suburban weekly popped up immediately, with a story saluting Rosy's retirement.

Rosy, I learned, had worked for General Motors in various Michigan manufacturing plants for forty years. He had held a minor volunteer position in his UAW local. Hmmm. He had been outdoor chairman of a Scout troop. Double hmmm. Could Rosy have followed me through the woods?

Rosy's wife, the article concluded, had worked for forty-five years as a 9-1-1 operator in suburban Detroit. Triple hmmm.

Rosy had retired five years earlier, and he had told the newspaper reporter he planned to move. He was quoted: "My wife and I want to get away from the city and live closer to nature." They'd certainly accomplished that. I read a few more articles about Nosy and Rosy, but that first one had the most information. Apparently their local rag hadn't done an article on Nosy when she retired.

The union activities and the police department connection were the only interesting things about Nosy and Rosy. I turned to Colonel Ace Smith.

At first I couldn't remember Ace's real first name. I finally took the simple expedient of looking in the Warner Pier phone book, and there was Rupert C. Smith III. It was that "III" that jogged my memory of Buzz being Somebody Smith IV.

I guess the Smith family might have skipped a generation of Ruperts. But apparently they hadn't. When I Googled him, Colonel Rupert C. Smith III showed up with a couple of thousand entries.

I looked at the pages of listings and marveled. Two thousand and eighteen listings? Wow! Maybe the guy didn't just think he was important. Maybe he really was.

Then I looked at the entry at the top of the list, thankful that Google ranks items in the order of popularity, and I gasped.

"Oh my gosh!" I yelled out. "Joe! Ace Smith was the Dobermann-Smith executive who was grilled by Congress two years ago!"

Joe called from the living room. "I knew that. I thought you did, too."

"No. I remember that the guy on the hot seat in the big scandal was a retired Colonel Smith, but I hadn't connected it with the Warner Pier Colonel Smith."

"Common last name."

Obviously Joe wasn't interested. But I was. I read on, reviewing what I knew about Colonel Smith and his problems with Congress.

Ace had been involved in one of those messy situations that may never be resolved. They hinge on differing views of governmental responsibilities and just what's a suitable — or legal — activity, in this case for a defense contractor.

Colonel Ace Smith had made it pretty clear where he stood on the question. He didn't give a darn what Congress said. He was going to do what was best for the country — not what he *thought* was best for the country. He was doing what *was* best for the country. Because what Colonel Ace Smith thought was right.

"He should have been court-martialed," I told myself.

"If he had still been in the army, he would have been," Joe said. I jumped. I hadn't heard him come into the room.

"Since he was retired from the army by then and was a partner in a company under contract to the army, it was harder to charge him," he said.

"Seems as if they could have gotten him for something."

"Not without taking down a couple of congressmen at the same time. I guess the congressmen had enough clout to keep that from happening."

"It was still a crime."

"It's a constitutional question," Joe said. "I agree with you. But I wouldn't want to be the one who had to argue it before the Supremes."

I read on, going over the testimony. It sounded as if Dobermann-Smith had set up a government of its own in a foreign country where the United States had a strong political and military presence. They'd been accused of doing everything from torture to theft to killing innocent people. The country itself was so disorganized that its citizens couldn't bring the Dobermann-Smith employees to justice. And because of the protection of a few powerful congressmen, the U.S. government hadn't been able to bring them to heel either.

This whole thing was tickling my memory — something about Buzz.

I quickly went to the *Warner Pier Gazette* Web page and looked up the stories about Buzz's death. There was a sidebar, a formal obituary. It hit the highlights of Buzz's life. It wasn't too long, of course. Buzz had been only twenty-four; he hadn't done much.

But what he had done was rather interesting. He had graduated from Midwest Military College. Then he had worked for the Dobermann-Smith Corporation for two years in a troubled eastern European country — the same one his dad had been quizzed about.

Very interesting.

After he had resigned from Dobermann-Smith Corporation, Buzz had come to Warner Pier and married Forsythia Hill. The next year she gave birth to John Smith. If Buzz had held another job, it wasn't mentioned.

Suddenly I wanted to know more about

Buzz Smith. I wondered if Sissy would be willing to talk about him.

CHAPTER 16

Yes, Sissy would be the best source for information about Buzz.

But was I brassy enough to quiz a widow about the character and activities of her murdered husband?

I considered that question. Actually, I probably was brassy enough for the job, I decided. But would it be wise?

I considered that question, too. No, it wouldn't, I also decided. Sissy might want to talk about Buzz of her own free will, but we weren't close enough that she would select me as a confidante.

I could talk to Wildflower. She had lived in the same household with Buzz. But somehow that smacked of going behind Sissy's back. I didn't like that idea either.

I chewed the idea over most of the night and clear through breakfast. Finally, shortly after nine the next morning, I walked into Sissy's office, closed the door behind me, sat down, and put four extra chocolate animals — two moose and two squirrels — on her desk.

"What's that?" Sissy said.

"A bribe, I guess. I'd like to talk to you."

"What have I done wrong?"

"Nothing at all. You're doing great. Considering the upsets of the past couple of days, I think it's a miracle you're still coming in for work."

"Then what did you want to talk about?"

"Put me down as a nosy bitch. And anytime you don't like the conversation, tell me to get out."

She reached over and took a moose. "This is much prettier than the moose we have at home. But you're making me nervous."

"I don't want to. I'm just trying to figure out a few things that are none of my business. Such as, when Buzz was killed, the investigators gave the public the impression that he had probably interrupted a burglar and the burglar reacted violently."

Sissy nodded. "That was what they seemed to think at first. But it was silly. Gran and I had nothing worth stealing, and Buzz didn't either. Maybe that was where the rumors about me being guilty came from."

"Why do you say that?"

"People look for a logical reason for things, I guess. Since theft didn't seem logical — nothing valuable was stolen from the house — they had to come up with another reason. And the husband or wife is always the first suspect. Plus, Ace hated me already, so he was willing to believe anything. He muttered to Helen, and she repeated his mutters." Sissy made an expressive gesture. "Next thing you knew, I was always first in the checkout line."

"First in the checkout line?"

"Yep. As soon as I was ready to check out, everyone else remembered some forgotten item and ran back to get it. So I got to go first. Unless they closed the line. That happened once or twice."

"Oh." I thought a minute, but I had nothing helpful to say about that. "Tell me about Buzz. I mean, what was he like? If you don't mind talking about him."

"I don't mind. I loved Buzz, and I love to talk about him. He was the nicest guy I ever knew. A real sweetheart. Not a mean bone in his body. His only problem, at least in my view, was that he liked to please people."

"How was that a problem?"

"It made him easy to push around. That's the real reason his dad hates me. Buzz always was a 'good boy.' Until I came along,

201

Buzz always minded his dad. Even when Ace packed him off to military school the week after his mother died."

"I didn't realize he did it that quickly. That seems pretty harsh."

"Not according to Ace. It was supposed to make a man of him. No mention was made of boarding school keeping him from being a bother to his dad."

"How old was Buzz?"

"Thirteen."

"Golly! Just a kid."

"Yes, I thought that was an awful thing to do. Of course, my influence on Buzz wasn't the only objection Ace had to the Hill family. We're a bit unconventional for him."

"You seem like nice folks to me."

"Oh, but my grandmother was a peace marcher! To Ace this was treason."

"I see."

"Ace was in Vietnam. I can understand how he felt — intellectually I understand it. I never expected him to be chums with my grandmother. But I resented his refusal even to think she held her opinions honestly. She was willing to give him the benefit of the doubt, but as far as he was concerned, she was unpatriotic, and that was that."

That was a quarrel that would never be settled. It was time to change the subject.

"How did you meet Buzz?"

"Oddly enough, Chip made the first overture. I had driven my old blue VW to the beach, and Chip and Buzz drove up in one almost exactly like it, except better kept. Chip leaned out the window and said, 'Hey! If we got our cars to breed, you could have pick of the litter.' "

"Oh gosh! What a line! How old were you all? I'd guess seventeen."

"Chip was probably nineteen. Seventeen mentally. Anyway, I glared and told him to get lost. After my friends and I had laid out our towels and had pranced around in our bikinis awhile, Buzz came over and made apologetic noises."

"Maybe it was a plan they had."

"I wouldn't put that past either of them. But I think Buzz was really afraid we'd tell Ace. About the car."

"Tell him what about the car?"

"Oh, Ace's blue Volkswagen was a collectible. It was his pride and joy. Chip and Buzz weren't supposed to drive it. Might get a scratch on it. Buzz didn't want us to say anything about their being in it. So we kept our mouths shut. But eventually Ace got rid of the VW, I think. I've never heard anything more about it."

"Did you begin dating Buzz then?"

"Not until the next summer. By then I was working as a waitress at the Sidewalk Café, and he used to come in. Of course, we ran into each other at the beach now and then. We were just pals for a couple of years, but we were dating before he went abroad.

"I really fell for him after he came back. That was when I began to understand how he'd been beaten down all his life. He was trying to deal with all that, to see that it was his dad who was at fault, to stop worshipping the jerk who had ruined his life. How could I not fall for him?"

Sissy clenched her jaw and made a fist. She rapped it on the desk a few times. Finally she gulped. "I keep trying to believe I've accepted Buzz's death, but when I think about it, I get furious all over again."

I leaned toward her. "I'm sorry! I shouldn't have been nosy. I won't pry again."

"No! No! Gran says I need to talk about it. But it's hard to think about the things Buzz went through growing up. And then later, there was all the stuff that went on overseas. Things he didn't want to talk about. Things that gave him nightmares. Finally, when he was able to break free from Ace and was beginning to get his life together — he was killed! For no reason anyone can see!"

She grabbed a box of tissues from her desk drawer, took one, and applied it to her nose.

"It's awful, Sissy." I reached over and took a tissue of my own.

We sat there and blubbered for a few minutes. I felt sure I had puffy eyes and mascara all over my face, but Sissy still looked beautiful.

"I only wish Buzz had finished his novel," she said.

"Buzz was writing a novel?"

"Yes. People around here think he just sat on his hands while Gran and I supported him, but he worked on it every day. We thought it was important, and that getting it done would help Buzz more than anything. We had enough money to get by on."

"What was it about?"

"I don't know any specifics. He didn't want to talk about it, and he didn't want me to read it."

"That seems odd. There's not much point in a novel unless it's read by other people."

"Buzz said he didn't want anyone to see it until it was 'fully formed.' And he didn't want to talk about it for the same reason."

"Did you read it after he died?"

"Didn't you hear? We've never found it."

"What do you mean?"

"I mean it had been erased from his computer, and all of his backups disappeared."

"Disappeared? Stolen?"

"We don't really know. He kept a box of thumb drives in his desk drawer. I had seen him copying things to those, but they were all blank."

"That could be a major clue!"

"The sheriff didn't think so. And I can't say he's wrong. If Buzz got disgusted with what he had written, he might well have erased it."

"And he never told you what the novel was about?"

"All he said was that it was therapeutic. I think he saw writing as a way to deal with the things that happened to him overseas. But he refused to tell me much about all that."

"Why? The counselor I saw — back during my divorce — told me that talking about bad stuff helps most of us deal with it."

"I think Buzz saw that as weakness." She shrugged. "Another part of the indoctrination he got from Ace. Besides, well, once Buzz did say that if I knew some of the things that went on over there, I might not love him anymore."

"How awful!"

Sissy and I each reached for another tissue. After we'd both dabbed our eyes and blown our noses, Sissy leaned forward. "Listen. If you really want to know about Buzz, Chip is the one to talk to. He knew him better than anybody did. They'd been friends since boarding school."

"And they're cousins?"

"Their dads were first cousins. But I don't think Chip and Buzz knew each other very well until they went away to military school. For college, they both tried for the service academies, but neither of them got in. So Ace saw that they went to a college with a strong military tradition."

"I see. But neither of them went into the military?"

"Right. That was also some idea Ace had." Sissy's voice took on a sarcastic tone. "He thought a man could do more for his country with Dobermann-Smith Corporation. He got them to go straight to being mercenaries."

"And after a couple of years of that, Buzz wanted to be a novelist?"

"As I said, I think it was his way of dealing with whatever happened overseas. He was very closemouthed about what was in the book. Though he may have opened up with Chip."

"But I thought Chip was still overseas then."

"He was, but they wrote each other all the time." Sissy gave a deep sigh. "I guess Chip knew Buzz better than I did. He'd certainly known him longer. And they'd had a lot of the same strange experiences."

I let Sissy get to work then, but when I got back to my own office, I stared at my computer screen blankly. Sissy's suggestion that I talk to Chip was a good one. But how could I do that?

I could use the same technique I used on Sissy — just ask him questions.

After all, Chip was staying with Ace, and Ace's number was in the telephone book.

I picked up the skinny little Warner County phone book. I noted that Colonel Rupert Smith had an address on Lake Shore Drive, not too far from where Joe and I lived. But while our house was on the inland side, the street number of the Smith cottage indicated it had a lake view. I thought it was in an area of larger homes built in the early 1900s. Of course, some of the houses in that area were simple cottages, but some were real mansions. Some sat on tiny lots, others on ten- or twenty-acre properties.

I wondered which category Ace's house fell into. I was willing to bet it was one of the larger places. After all, Helen Ferguson had rented a house on the property, and Ace was prepared to live there year-round. That indicated the house was winterized and wasn't on a small lot. Lakeside property of any size, and with two year-round houses, would be worth quite a bit in Warner Pier. Even if Chip didn't tell me anything, it would be interesting to see the house.

I picked up the phone and called.

Ace answered, his voice gruff. I asked for Chip in my most businesslike voice, hoping I sounded like a dentist's office or some other business, and Ace didn't ask me for a name.

After a moment, a different voice came on the line. "This is Chip Smith."

"Hi, Chip. This is Lee Woodyard."

Chip gasped. "Oh! Hi."

"I wanted to ask you a few questions —"

"Listen. I never have looked up those figures. Let me get them, and I'll call you right back."

"What?"

"It'll only be a few minutes."

Click. He hung up.

I stared at the phone in disbelief. Chip had hung up on me? And what figures had he thought I wanted? His response had been nonsensical.

I had realized he might not want to talk to me, but I had expected him to give me a chance to explain why I called.

Crazy. What was going on?

I considered calling back, but it seemed pointless. Instead, I tried to concentrate on my own work. I'd been neglecting it lately. Luckily, I had a lenient boss.

Maybe Chip really would call back.

And sure enough, five minutes later the phone rang, and my "TenHuis Chocolade" greeting was answered with a voice that was almost a whisper.

"Lee Woodyard?"

"Yes."

"It's Chip Smith. Sorry I couldn't talk when you called a few minutes ago. Things were a bit crowded."

"Crowded?"

"Yes. Ace was standing right beside me."

"Oh? I just had a few questions for you. Could I talk you into meeting me for lunch?"

"Lunch?" Chip sounded as if he'd never heard of the meal.

"Yes. I thought we could go to the Side-walk Café."

"Oh." That required more thought. "I'll

be happy to meet you. But maybe not in Warner Pier."

"Oh?" Now it was my turn to sound surprised — largely because I was.

"How about the General Store?" Chip said.

"You mean the one at Willard?"

"Yes. I could pick you up."

"No, I can get myself there. What time?"

"One o'clock? It's never crowded."

"I guess not." There was a reason the General Store in Willard was never crowded. The place had a reputation for really lousy food.

"It ought to be a quiet place to talk," I said. "I'll meet you there."

"Fine. One o'clock." Chip hung up.

I hung up, too. What the heck had I done? I'd just agreed to meet a guy who knew two murder victims, and to meet him in a secluded place and at a time when that place would be almost deserted. And I had agreed to meet him alone.

I must be crazy.

I picked up the phone, ready to call and cancel.

Then I reminded myself that Chip hadn't even been mentioned in the investigation of Buzz's death.

I punched the numbers that rang Sissy's

phone. "Hey, it's Lee. Sissy, was Chip around when Buzz died?"

"No. He called me from someplace. Bosnia? Or Afghanistan? Honestly, I don't remember. But it was someplace far away."

"Thanks."

So Chip had been out of the country when Buzz died. He hadn't been a suspect. But how about Helen Ferguson? Could he be a suspect in her death?

Maybe, maybe not. But working on Rosy Reagan's suspicion that the prowler of last February was the same prowler who had left tracks at Nosy and Rosy's house — well, Chip couldn't have been the first prowler, so he must not have been the second.

It was still stupid for me to meet him at the Willard General Store — alone, at least.

I picked up the phone again. Time to call in my personal knight in shining armor. Thank goodness this was a day when Joe worked at the boat shop, not thirty miles away as a lawyer.

Joe answered on the first ring.

"How about lunch?" I said.

"Sure."

"Great! And how's your white steed doing?"

"He's fine. Do you want me to ride him?"

"Please."

Joe laughed. "Okay, Lee. What kind of mess have you gotten into this time?"

CHAPTER 17

When Joe and I got to the Willard General Store, I spotted a rental car parked in front. It was small and a flashy yellow; it had probably been the least desirable car in the leasing company's lot. I recognized it as a rental by the sticker on the back bumper.

I pointed to the car. "I guess Chip is already here."

"I'm surprised he agreed to talk to you about Buzz," Joe said.

I stopped walking. "You know, he didn't even ask what I wanted to talk about."

Joe frowned. "You mean he wanted to meet you way out here to talk, and he didn't even wonder why?"

"That's right. I just realized it."

"That's nuts."

"I agree."

"No wonder your subconscious was telling you something was crazy. That something may be Chip, and you may well be better off not coming alone. Maybe I should have brought my brass knuckles."

Joe took my hand, and we headed inside.

For at least a minute I couldn't find Chip. The Willard General Store wasn't exactly brightly lighted.

I couldn't remember ever being there before, though of course I knew it existed. The store is one of those hangovers from earlier rural life, a convenience store serving a small specific community. Willard is a clump of maybe two dozen houses, rather than a town or village. I'm sure it's not incorporated. The Willard school was probably absorbed by Warner Pier as soon as the school bus was invented. There's one small church, but no restaurant, post office, or other meeting place.

The Willard General Store is the only place there to buy gasoline or a loaf of bread or — well, anything. Five miles west of the community are an up-to-date service station and convenience store that cater to the interstate traffic, but Willard itself remains isolated.

Inside, the store was probably forty feet long and thirty feet wide, and it was crowded with shelves. As we walked through, I spotted rifle shells — lots of deer hunters around here — motor oil, bubble gum, Hershey Bars, fishing lures, miniature sewing kits, garden rakes, white socks, canned goods, pantyhose, and a large supply of beer — and a thousand other items.

At the back of the store was an old-fashioned meat counter, not too large, holding deli meats and cheeses. On the worn wooden floor in front of it were three Formica-topped kitchen tables that looked as if they'd been picked up at garage sales. Behind the tables were two glass-fronted refrigerators loaded with milk and soft drinks.

The whole place was so dimly lighted I barely recognized Chip, who was sitting at the table farthest from the meat cooler. When he stood up, I saw the table tip over about an inch. I couldn't tell if the table had a short leg or if the floor was uneven.

"Hi!" I said. I walked close to him and spoke quietly. "How'd you find this place?"

"Originally? Buzz guided me here." Chip smiled nervously and lowered his own voice. "They used to be real lax about checking IDs. All the high school guys we knew came out here to buy beer."

"Fascinating variety of stock."

"You should have seen it last February. Believe it or not, they moved everything around so they could paint. It was the biggest mishmash in the history of the world."

Joe and I turned back to the counter, where a plain girl with a lot of large teeth stood ready to take orders for food. I decided on a cheese sandwich; the General Store's deli meats didn't look particularly fresh. Chip already had a sandwich and a Bud. Before he sat down again, he went to a rack displaying individual sacks of chips and pulled down some Fritos. You waited on yourself at the Willard General Store.

At least the service was quick. In about two minutes Joe and I had our sandwiches, had taken chips from the hanging rack, and had pulled Cokes from the cooler. Chip grinned as we sat down at the uneven table. "If I keep my elbows on the table," he said, "your drinks won't tip over. And Ace isn't here to scold me about my table manners."

We all bit into our sandwiches. The cheese I'd ordered was strongly flavored, better than I'd expected.

I saw that Chip was eyeing me, apparently waiting for me to speak. So I did. "Why did you want to come all the way out here to talk, Chip?"

"I thought it would be a good place for a private conversation." He flashed that boyish grin again. "And I thought Ace wouldn't find out that we'd gotten together."

217

"Is that important?"

"He has a lot of clout with my boss. And I have to head back to duty in two weeks."

"Why wouldn't Ace want you to talk to me?"

"Because you're friends with Sissy and her grandmother."

"So are you, Chip. Or you act as if you'd like to be friends with them."

"I do like Sissy. And Wildflower. But — well, Ace will never forgive Wildflower for being antiwar. You know, peace marches and so on forty or fifty years ago. And he considers Sissy part of the same culture."

I took another bite, then chewed and swallowed his comment along with my bread and cheese. "Actually," I said, "I didn't want to talk about Sissy. I had something else on my mind."

"I know, I know! It was a crazy situation, and I handled it all wrong."

Huh? If my mouth hadn't been full, I would have let it gape open. What was Chip talking about?

He didn't go on, so I did. "I don't know what situation you're talking about. I only wanted to find out something about Buzz."

"Buzz? Oh." He sounded amazed.

"Yes. What did you think I wanted to talk about?"

Chip occupied himself with opening his Fritos before he answered. "I didn't really know. But I'll be glad to talk about Buzz. He was a great guy. I'll never get over his . . . what happened to him. What did you want to know?"

"How long had you known Buzz?"

"Our dads were cousins, but we hadn't met until he started military school. We weren't roommates every year, but we always lived in the same dorm. Then in college we roomed together for three years."

"What kind of a guy was Buzz?"

"Deep." Chip said the word without hesitation. He stopped and thought before he went on. "Yeah. Deep is the right word. Buzz couldn't just slough things off. He buried them inside. Where they bother you the most."

"Sissy said he was the nicest guy she ever knew."

"He was when he was around her."

"But not around you?"

"Oh, Buzz was always a great guy. He had a lot of heart, I guess. When we were in — when we were overseas, he tamed a stray dog. You know, fed it. Named the dog Nero. But he didn't always think ahead. Like the deal with the dog. When we left, he couldn't take the dog along. There was no one over there to take it in. So he'd gotten the dog used to being taken care of, then he was going to have to abandon it."

"How awful! The poor dog could have starved."

"No. He made sure that didn't happen."

"How could he manage that?"

"Oh, he handled the situation."

"How?"

Joe spoke for the first time. "Did he have to dispose of the dog?"

"Oh no. He paid someone to take him in." Chip ducked his head and stared at his sandwich. "Left some money for feeding him. Asked me to check on the situation."

"Did the people take care of Nero?"

"As near as I could tell." Now Chip was staring at the nearest shelf. It held a selection of garden tools. He didn't seem real confident that Buzz's solution for Nero had worked. Joe shook his head at me, and I decided it was best not to pursue it further.

"How'd Buzz get along with the guys y'all worked with?"

"Okay."

"I'd have thought they would be a rough bunch. Hard for a 'deep' guy to handle."

Chip shrugged. "There was a certain amount of hazing in the unit. But Buzz had learned to deal with that at military school.

In fact, once he made a crack — something about 'just like eighth grade.' It didn't go over very well. But his dad was an executive of the company, after all. Nobody messed with him much."

I tried a different tack. "Were you surprised when Buzz and Sissy got married?"

"No. They'd been nuts about each other for a couple of years. Buzz just had to make the break with his dad before it could happen. After he finished his tour overseas, he said he was going to quit his job. He said his dad was asking too much of him. He just hated it all."

"All?"

"It's rough over there. You have to compartmentalize your life. You do what the job requires, and you don't let it affect you." Chip shrugged. "That's the way to get along. Of course, Buzz wasn't made that way. Ace should have realized it."

"How did Buzz react to his dad's testimony before Congress?"

"He hated it. Ace still thinks everything he did was right, you know. He isn't a bad guy. He's the most patriotic guy in the world. Buzz was split right down the middle — embarrassed for his dad, but he understood where Ace's critics were coming from, too. And that bunch of liberals made him look like a traitor."

Hmmm. I hadn't known I was one of "a bunch of liberals." Giving private political ideas priority over the instructions of the U.S. Congress didn't strike me as particularly patriotic, and that was apparently what Ace Smith had done. However, I didn't want to get sidetracked into a discussion on political ethics. I bit into my sandwich, glad of the excuse to shut up for a moment.

Chip had described Buzz as a person who was bothered by the things that went on while he was working for Dobermann-Smith Corporation. His dad's testimony must have bothered him even more. I chewed, swallowed, and felt sorry for Buzz. Then I spoke again.

"What about Buzz's novel?"

"Novel?" Chip's voice was completely innocent. "What novel?"

"The novel he was writing."

"Huh?"

"You didn't know about it? Sissy thought you and Buzz exchanged letters about it."

"No! I didn't know anything about Buzz writing a novel."

I was incredulous. "But Sissy was sure . . ."

"No." Chip's denial was firm. "I didn't know anything about a novel. I can't imagine Buzz writing a book."

222

Well, I could. Based on Chip's own account of his personality, Buzz had been an introspective person who absorbed unhappy experiences. "He buried them inside, where they bother you the most," Chip had said. It occurred to me that Chip might have a few things buried inside, too.

And when unhappy experiences are buried inside, the creative process is one way to get them out. I could see a counselor advising Buzz to write about the things that bothered him. Of course, I had no idea that Buzz had ever seen any sort of counselor, even though it sounded as if he needed one. But writing a novel might have been a therapeutic experience for him.

I was concentrating on this topic so hard that I was surprised when Joe spoke, asking Chip some innocuous question. When he had to return to duty, I think. Or maybe how often he got leave. I was so surprised by Chip's flat denial that he knew anything about Buzz's novel that I hardly listened.

We finished our lunch with ice cream bars. I was still quiet. My mind was racing, but Chip had stonewalled me completely by denying that he knew anything about Buzz's novel.

Joe and I were on our way back to Warner Pier before I had any significant comment.

"He lied," I said. "Chip lied about the novel."

"Probably," Joe said.

"Why?"

"Because he didn't want to talk about it."

"Duh! Why not?"

"Oh, I expect you could come up with some speculation on that point."

I sighed. "I'd guess that whether or not Chip knows what's in the novel, he thinks it's too hot to handle. He doesn't want anyone — for 'anyone,' read 'Ace' — to find out he knows about the novel."

"And Sissy says Buzz wouldn't tell her anything about his book?"

"No. And he wouldn't let either her or Wildflower read any of it."

"And the manuscript disappeared?"

"That's what Sissy told me. Of course, it wasn't on paper. But there was no file with a novel on it in Buzz's computer. And the thumb drives he used to back up his files were blank."

"It sounds as if the person who shot Buzz raided his computer."

"It sounds like it to me, too, but Sissy said the sheriff wasn't convinced."

"I think Ramsey got stuck on the idea that Sissy had a lover and wanted to get rid of Buzz. He didn't really look at any other possibility."

"What does Hogan think?"

"He's not tipping his hand. Especially since Helen Ferguson was killed in his jurisdiction, not Ramsey's."

"And I guess he thinks the two killings are connected."

"They're both connected to Ace Smith. Maybe to Sissy." We left it at that.

Joe didn't fight the Warner Pier summer season traffic for a parking place. He just dropped me in front of TenHuis Chocolade, and I ran in the door.

As soon as I was inside, I heard a woman yelling.

"Because of you my mom is dead! I'll see that you get what's coming to you if it's the last thing I do!"

Somebody was in the back room screaming. I ran through the retail shop and skidded to a stop in the workroom.

A young woman with brassy blond hair was standing in the door to Sissy's office. And she was yelling.

"You can't just go around killing people who get in your way! I'm going to see that you suffer for this!"

CHAPTER 18

Mom. The angry woman had used the word *mom.* And she was accusing Sissy of killing someone.

This must be Helen Ferguson's daughter.

I had forgotten that Helen had a daughter, so her identity hadn't slapped me in the eye. Now I remembered that Sissy had said Helen tried to promote her own daughter as a romantic partner for Buzz.

Maybe I'd learned a lesson by yelling at the sheriff. This time I vowed to keep my voice low and my temper cool.

The young woman was well inside Sissy's door, so I managed to slip in and move around in front of her. From her viewpoint, I must have jumped up like a jack-in-the-box. She gasped and stopped talking.

"Hello," I said. "I'm Lee Woodyard. I'm business manager for TenHuis Chocolade. Please come around to my office."

The woman pouted. "I was talking to

Sissy. I don't need to talk to you."

"Perhaps not. But I need to have Sissy on the job. Personal matters will have to wait until she's on her own time."

"Oh." The word had an offended edge.

"Everyone who comes into TenHuis receives a sample chocolate," I said. "Just come with me, and I'll get you one."

Who can resist chocolate? She followed me into the shop. But she balked at selecting a chocolate.

"I guess I shouldn't have come," she said. "You don't need to give me chocolate." The words were polite, but the tone was whiny.

"As I said, we give every visitor a sample bonbon or truffle. Would you like a cappuccino truffle? They're milk chocolate inside and out, with a creamy flavor that hints at coffee. Or how about something a bit more exotic? We have rosemary truffles. The interiors have a trace of rosemary in white chocolate ganache, and they're covered in dark chocolate and embellished with dried rosemary."

"No! I'd better get out of here. You're all on Sissy's side."

As the old saying goes, I didn't want her to go away mad. I just wanted her to go away. She headed for the door, and I followed, catching up with her on the sidewalk.

"I don't know your name," I said.

"Why should you? Nobody ever noticed me when Sissy was around. My name is Fran Park. It used to be Fran Ferguson."

"Then you're Helen Ferguson's daughter. I'm terribly sorry about your mother."

Tears welled in her eyes. "She wasn't an easy person to get along with, but she was my mother."

All I could do was nod. She'd just described my relationship with my own mother. Heaven knows we've had our problems, but she's still my mom.

"It just seems so awful for her to be killed," Fran said. "Then thrown down that stairway. Just left there!" She turned back toward our shop, and I thought she was going to shake a fist.

The situation wasn't improving. I had thought it was a good thing to get Helen Ferguson's daughter out of TenHuis Chocolade, but if she stood outside and made a scene, it was going to be worse. I needed to get her away from the public eye.

I tried to use a soothing voice. "Fran, let's go down to the Sidewalk Café. They have a back room where we can get a cup of coffee."

I almost expected Fran to storm off, but she again followed along. I was beginning to think she wanted someone to boss her a bit. Well, that was something I was good at, or so my friends were always telling me.

I herded Fran, who was still weeping, for half a block, until we reached the Sidewalk Café. Luckily, my close friend Lindy Herrera was managing the restaurant for her father-in-law, and she was on duty. When I came in with a weeping woman, she was happy to whisk us out of sight of the main dining room, tucking us into the back room usually reserved for private parties. She promised to bring us coffee and left us alone, closing the door behind herself.

Between sobs Fran continued to whine. "It's just such a shock. The last time I talked to Mom, she was so happy."

"I met your mother only once, but she struck me as an upbeat person." Or she pretended to be. I didn't say that aloud, of course.

"And she had just arranged a good business deal."

"Oh? What sort of business?"

"She didn't tell me. But she said they were close to an agreement, and it would be a good deal for her. Then for that awful Sissy to kill her!"

"But what makes you think Sissy killed your mother?"

"She killed her husband, and my mom knew it."

"But the authorities —"

"Oh, Sissy's always gotten her own way! Ever since grade school. Everybody thought she was so cute, she couldn't do anything wrong. But I was in her class for twelve years, and, believe me, she did plenty wrong! Then she killed Buzz! And now my mom. And she'll get away with it! She must have that police chief wrapped right around her finger. Innocent for reasons of cuteness!"

"Okay! Okay!" I wanted to calm Fran down, not inflame her. "But as I understand it, the police think your mom was killed by one blow, probably from a stick or club. And they think she wasn't killed at the beach, but somewhere else. Then she was carried to the beach and thrown down the steps. Do you think Sissy is strong enough to do that?"

A frown crossed Fran's face. "If she were really angry, maybe."

"Could you do it? I don't think I could. And we're each as strong as Sissy."

"Sissy could have hit her." Fran's face brightened. "She could have used a stick. Or a jack handle. And she could have used a wheelbarrow to move her."

"An adult is still pretty heavy. Did the police tell you they'd found evidence of a wheelbarrow being at the beach? Tracks, maybe?"

"No. They didn't tell me anything." She was still whining.

"Then maybe you'd better wait until you talk to them before you make up your mind. I know they questioned Sissy twice, because she found your mom, but they haven't seemed interested in charging her."

Fran sighed deeply. Her attitude seemed to have moved from grief to martyrdom. "It's just that it would be so logical if Sissy killed my mom. Because my mom was the only one who could link Sissy to the Volkswagen."

"The Volkswagen? The one Sissy drives?"

"Yes. The Volkswagen that was supposedly in the shop. The one that was seen out near Moose Lodge the day Buzz Smith was shot to death."

My first impulse was to roll my eyes. There was that old story again — the one about someone, the indefinite someone, who saw Sissy's Volkswagen driving toward Moose Lodge at the same time a dozen witnesses had said she was in Holland.

But out of respect for Fran's grief, I simply dropped my eyes and tried to hide my reaction.

This didn't please Fran. "I can see you think I'm lying. Well, I'm not!"

"I know a lot of people believe that story, Fran. But the detectives talked to the garage owner in Holland, and he swore Sissy's VW was in the shop over the whole weekend."

"Then he's lying. Or he didn't notice it was gone."

"I've been told about the Volkswagen several times, but when you try to pin people down, the story always dissolves."

"What do you mean?"

"I mean you can never find the person who actually saw the Volkswagen. It's always a friend of a friend. Or someone's cousin's aunt's next-door neighbor. Anyway, the tale can never be traced down to prove the truth of it."

"But my mom did see the car." Fran leaned forward and spoke eagerly. "It was right after Colonel Smith moved his stuff into his family place, see. He'd gone to Florida for a couple of weeks, and Mom was clearing up the house. She took a load of boxes out to the dump. And there was this Volkswagen on the road in front of her."

"Was it Sissy's Volkswagen?"

"I admit she didn't see who was driving it. And she didn't write down the license number. I mean, why should she? She just thought it was Sissy going home. She didn't know Sissy was headed out there to kill her husband. But she saw a Volkswagen, and it was headed for Moose Lodge."

"Did your mother tell the investigators about this?"

Fran sat back and folded her arms. "Colonel Smith didn't want her to."

"That's hard to believe. He's acted as if he thinks Sissy is guilty."

"I can't explain it. I only know that's what my mother told me."

"Have you told the authorities about it?"

Fran dropped her eyes, then looked at me from under her lashes. "No. I haven't told them yet."

"Why on earth not?"

The eyelashes fluttered. "Well, if Mom thought she should hold off because Colonel Smith asked her to . . . And I thought I ought to talk to him before I told. I mean, the story is bound to hurt Sissy. He might not like that." Flutter, flutter went the lashes.

Then Fran looked directly at me and spoke. "For that matter, you might not like it. None of Sissy's friends are likely to want the story told."

Fran gave me a really innocent look. Was

she trying to get me to give her some sort of payoff? Had her mom blackmailed Sissy? Was Fran trying to blackmail me?

For at least a full minute I considered what she'd said. Yes, I believed Sissy was innocent of her husband's murder. I believed she was innocent of Helen Ferguson's murder, for that matter. No, I didn't want more talk around town about how Sissy could have killed either of them.

But I wasn't hiding behind Wildflower's couch when Buzz was shot. I wasn't behind a bush at Beech Tree Beach when someone threw Helen Ferguson's body down the stairs. I had no idea what happened to either of them.

I believed in Sissy, but I didn't want to hide evidence.

Suddenly, I'd fooled around with Fran Ferguson Whatever-her-name-was long enough. I was tired of her.

Luckily, I had my cell phone in my pocket. I pulled it out and punched the button for the Warner Pier Police Department. Hogan's secretary answered.

I stared Fran right in the eye as I spoke into the phone. "This is Lee Woodyard," I said. "Please tell Hogan that I'm in the back room at the Sidewalk Café. Fran Ferguson is with me. She says her mother told her

234

something that might be important. It's about the day Buzz Smith was killed. I'd appreciate it if Hogan or some other officer would come right over here and let her tell them about it."

Fran jumped to her feet. "I'm not talking to the cops!"

"She's threatening to leave," I told the cell phone calmly. I listened. Then I turned to Fran. "They said to tell you it would look very bad if you don't stick around until someone comes to talk to you."

I lied. Actually, Hogan's secretary hadn't said anything of the sort. She had merely said she'd try to have someone there quickly.

Fran might have fled the scene if it hadn't been for Lindy. Fran headed for the door, but when she opened it, Lindy was standing there with two mugs and a carafe of coffee.

"Sorry it took me so long," she said. "Hogan and Jerry Cherry came in, and I stopped to talk to them for a minute."

I laughed. That's the joy of living in a small town. Coincidences happen all the time. Actually, I should have remembered that Hogan always met with his night patrolman sometime in the middle of the afternoon, and they often came to the Sidewalk Café for a cup of coffee and a piece of pie while they talked.

So Fran was still standing there, probably trying to make up a story that would explain what she'd said to me, when Hogan and Jerry left their midafternoon snack and came into the room.

I immediately went back to my office.

I was torn emotionally. Fran had offered me the chance to shut her mouth, and that might have protected Sissy from further suspicion. But it wouldn't have protected her in the long run. And if Sissy really had driven her old Volkswagen in the vicinity of Moose Lodge the day Buzz was killed, well, maybe it needed to come out.

When I got to my office, I threw myself into my chair, and almost immediately someone came in the door. It was Sissy, of course.

"Thanks for taking Fran away," she said, "but if you'd waited another five minutes, I could have sued her for slander."

"Oh, you can still sue her. I got her to a less public place, but she kept up the bad-mouthing."

"I'm sorry you got stuck with her."

I waved at my chair. "I guess we have to cut her some slack. She may not be a very nice person, but she did lose her mother tragically. I'm afraid you're not going to like the way I handled it."

I took a deep breath and repeated the story Fran had told, identifying her mother as the person who claimed to have seen the Volkswagen near Moose Lodge.

Sissy nodded. "Helen told me she had seen me out there. She seemed to think I would beg her not to tell. Maybe offer her money. I didn't. I just told her I didn't kill Buzz, and she should do whatever she thought was right."

"I had wondered if Helen had tried to blackmail you. I thought Fran was close to asking for hush money."

"I don't have any money — hush or any other kind. All I did was urge Helen to go to the sheriff."

"Did you report her threats to the sheriff yourself?"

"I should have. But by the time she approached me, Sheriff Ramsey and I weren't speaking."

"Did the investigators search your car?"

"I gave them permission to search it. Whether they did or not, I don't know. I was in such a daze then . . ."

She stood up. "Guess I'll try to do a little work. And a little is all I seem to get done around here. Sorry."

I checked the time on my computer screen. So much had happened that afternoon that I felt as if it were quitting time, but it was only three o'clock. I tried to get to work, too.

Of course, I kept eyeing the front door. But Hogan didn't come by to pick up Sissy.

In fact, the main thing that happened that afternoon was rain. About four thirty, it began to pour. There's nothing unexpected about that, of course. Michigan gets rain, even in July. That's okay with us merchants, because when the tourists can't go to the beach, they hit Warner Pier's quaint downtown, looking for clothes, food, and souvenirs.

The only problem with rain is that at five o'clock, when the ladies who make our chocolate and the two of us who handle the money — Sissy and I — leave, we have to do so in the rain. And that day had started out sunny and beautiful, so no one had brought a raincoat or umbrella. Plus, most workers in downtown businesses park in that special lot several blocks away where they can use a reserved section. So the downpour caused cries of consternation from people who thought they were going to have to walk several blocks in a driving rain with no rain gear.

I could hear what was going on, so I went back to the shop. "Hey! My van's in the

238

back alley. I can get at least six in, and I'll give y'all lifts to the parking lot. I can make two trips — or even three."

My offer was accepted. The crew decided who should have the rides. It finally boiled down to two loads of women who needed lifts to the parking lot.

Sissy said she'd take the second trip and try to finish up one project before she left. "As long as I pick Johnny up by five thirty, I'm okay," she said.

When I honked in the alley and the second six ran out for their ride, Sissy came out holding several file folders wrapped in a plastic bag. "I can't stay because I have to pick Johnny up," she said, "but I can finish this tonight."

"Well, okay. But keep track of your hours."

I dropped everybody off in the parking lot with the rain still teeming down. Sissy was last, and I pulled up in front of her old blue Volkswagen. She'd already jumped into her car when I realized she'd left her package in the van.

"Wait!" I yelled, but I knew she couldn't hear me, so I honked. I reached for the package from the backseat and waved it at her. Then I jumped out of my van, splashed over to the passenger side of Sissy's car, and opened the door.

"If I'm going to exploit the help, you'd better have this."

I slammed the door. Maybe I slammed it too hard, because the door to her glove compartment flew open.

And an automatic pistol fell out and landed on the floor.

I stared at it in shocked silence. It was Sissy who spoke. I could hear her even with the window rolled up.

"What the heck is Buzz's pistol doing there?"

CHOCOLATE CHAT

The veterinary clinic in our neighborhood had the following sign on its message board before Christmas:

CHOCOLATE IS FOR YOUR VET, NOT YOUR PET.

Yes, chocolate can be poison to dogs.

Keep it away from them. And if they get into it, call the vet. He or she may advise you to induce vomiting or to bring them to the clinic.

A lot depends on the size of the dog and, of course, on how much chocolate the animal eats, as well as on the type of chocolate. A large dog may gobble up a large amount and not be injured, but a small dog may find a small amount fatal. Dark chocolate is more dangerous than milk chocolate.

Symptoms of chocolate poisoning include hyperactivity, muscle twitching, increased urination, and excessive panting. Seizures could follow. Effects should go away in less than two days.

Cats are generally affected less severely, but chocolate is still poisonous to them.

CHAPTER 19

I stood there, with the rain running down my face, and the memory that flashed through my mind was Rosy Reagan saying that Wildflower refused to have a gun around Moose Lodge.

But now Sissy said this was Buzz's pistol. How did she know? Where had it come from? Why was it in Sissy's car?

And, most important, was it the weapon that killed Buzz?

Sissy closed her eyes and rested her head on the steering wheel of the VW. I reopened the door.

"You seem surprised by the pistol, Sissy. Did you know it was in the glove box?"

"I have no idea how it got in my car. The cops are going to go nuts over this."

"I'm afraid you're right. But they need to know."

She spoke dully. "I knew you'd say that."

I stood there, wondering what she meant.

Did she mean I was right? Or did she mean my remark demonstrated my character and personality? Did she agree with me? Or did she think I was bossing her around?

Or did she mean she could have quietly disposed of the pistol if I hadn't witnessed its appearance?

Sissy didn't explain what she'd meant, but she sat up straight and gave a deep sigh. "This isn't real convenient," she said. "It sure would have been better to find the gun around noon, when I wasn't in a rush to pick Johnny up. I'll call and get my grandmother to take care of that."

Then she gave me a glance that was awfully close to a dirty look. "You can call your pal Hogan. And for goodness' sake, Lee, get out of the rain!"

I got back in the van and called Hogan. He gave a low whistle at the news. "I'll be right over," he said.

"I sure hope you won't have to get that sheriff involved," I said.

"I'll call the state detectives who were involved in the investigation of Buzz's death. They can handle him. Just stay there until I come."

When I motioned for Sissy to join me in my van, she shook her head, so the two of us sat there, each isolated in her own vehicle in the driving rain. Not that either of us had anything to say to the other.

The Warner Pier cops arrived in five minutes. Then Hogan moved Sissy to a patrol car and had her driven to the police department. He told me to follow. I had called Joe by then, and he met us at the station.

Bless Joe's heart; he brought us two cups of hot chocolate from the Warner Pier Coffeehouse.

We sat in the PD's reception area and said nothing. I felt as low as I'd ever felt in my life, and Sissy seemed to feel even lower. Even hot chocolate wasn't any real comfort.

Joe didn't ask Sissy any questions, and she volunteered only one remark to him.

"Joe, if I had known that pistol was in the glove box, it wouldn't have been there very long. Between Moose Lodge and Warner Pier there are a million bushes I could have tossed it behind. Plus, I would never have hidden it there in the first place. The glove compartment door is broken. It falls open at the slightest excuse."

"I didn't think you knew about it, Sissy. You're not stupid."

The three of us sat there in silence for forty-five minutes. Waiting. And — in my case at least — worrying.

All sorts of wild suspicions were charging around in my head. Had Sissy known the gun was in the glove box? She said she hadn't, but if I hadn't been there when the gun fell out, it would have been very simple for her to make it disappear again. Would she have done that?

Heaven knows that in her place I would have been tempted to do exactly that.

On the other hand, the glove box was — as Joe had said — a really stupid place to hide the gun. It wasn't really hidden at all. Anyone might look in there. And I hadn't done anything unusual to make the door fall open and the gun fall out. That made it seem more like a plant.

Supposing that someone — Buzz's killer? — had planted the gun in Sissy's car, when had the person done it? Of course, her car had been sitting in the parking lot all day. There was an attendant at the lot, but his main function was to guide the tourists to parking slots. People walked around the lot all day and all evening: tourists, employees of Warner Pier businesses, deliverymen — everybody.

And I'd driven enough old cars to know they're easy to break into. The traditional Slim Jim won't open a new-model car, but it works like a charm on an older one.

I gave a gasp. "Sissy! When I came up to the passenger side of your car, did you unlock the door for me?"

"No. I reached over to roll the window down, but you opened the door before I could do it."

"Then that door was already unlocked."

Sissy sat forward. "It shouldn't have been. I'm sure I left the car locked this morning."

After a moment she spoke again. "Not that it really matters."

What did she mean by that?

The three of us settled back into our brown studies.

It looked as if somebody had unlocked the door to Sissy's car sometime during the day. At least that was one point on her side.

But why did I feel that Sissy needed a point on her side? Was I doubting her innocence?

Hogan came in then, and I quickly made a statement, explaining why I had driven Sissy to her car, why I had opened the passenger door, and what I had seen. Then Hogan — and Joe — instructed me to go home.

Instead, I went over to Aunt Nettie's and told her all about it.

She listened patiently, because that's what she does. Then I sat back and waited for reassurance. Aunt Nettie would surely erase all my doubts about Sissy. She would tell me that Sissy was innocent as the proverbial driven snow on the convent roof and that Hogan would prove it. Sissy would be back home in time to put little Johnny to bed.

And, sure enough, Aunt Nettie spoke calmly. "Well, Lee, we'll just have to wait and see."

That wasn't the reassuring answer I'd been waiting for.

"But I feel as if I should do something!" I said.

"I don't think there's anything to be done. Hogan is a fair investigator. He'll do his best to find out how the gun got there."

"I know."

"In the meantime, you need to distance yourself from the situation a bit."

"What do you mean?"

"I mean that I've supervised a group of women for more than thirty years, and it's hard not to lose your objectivity about them — particularly about ones you like. Or about ones you don't like. I think it's called 'emotional investment.' "

"Yes, you're right."

"Sissy is a very appealing young woman. She has a knack for making people want to take care of her."

"Helen Ferguson's daughter says she's

always gotten away with things because she's cute."

"Yes, even Hogan has noticed it. He told me he had to guard against wanting to prove Sissy innocent, instead of wanting to discover the facts. And Hogan can be pretty cynical about people involved in murder cases."

Aunt Nettie smiled. "So, Joe will see that Sissy has proper legal representation. And Hogan will see that her situation is investigated fairly."

She shook her finger at me. "And you and I will keep out of it."

I laughed a little. "Yes, Aunt Nettie."

"Now, I put some spaghetti sauce in the slow cooker this morning. How about we all plan to have dinner together?"

"Assuming that Joe and Hogan ever get away from the police station. I'll make salad."

I was still worried. Aunt Nettie had offered practical advice, but she had missed the point of my concern about Sissy. I wasn't concerned because I thought Sissy was being treated unjustly. I was worried because for the first time I recognized the possibility that she was guilty.

Maybe Sissy could actually have killed her husband. Maybe she could have killed

Helen Ferguson. Neither action seemed likely, but, for the first time, neither seemed impossible.

Aunt Nettie and I concerned ourselves with dinner, and in about an hour Joe called, asking if I could go along while he gave Sissy a ride home. So they hadn't arrested her. But the lab guys wanted to keep her car overnight.

I didn't know if I was to be a chaperone or a witness on this trip.

When I walked into the police station, the first person I saw was Ace. I steeled myself for a scene. Every time I'd observed Ace and Sissy together, there had been yelling and screaming. I'd blamed Ace, but when he attacked, Sissy had certainly given as good as she got.

This time things were different. Ace was talking to Hogan, and he was talking quietly. "Here are the numbers you asked for," he said.

"Thanks, Colonel Smith. This should be what we need to ID the pistol."

"May I see it?"

"Yes, though I can't let you touch it."

"I understand." Ace sounded unbelievably reasonable. I wondered what he was up to.

Hogan led Ace over to a table at the back of the room, and I turned to Sissy, who was still sitting in the reception area. "Ready to go?"

"Let's wait a minute. I'm beginning to feel at home here."

I didn't understand why Sissy wanted to stay, but I didn't argue. I sat down beside her. "Where's Joe?"

"He went into one of the offices to make a phone call."

By then it was nearly eight o'clock. Sissy looked worn out. Neither of us said anything, and we could hear Ace and Hogan clearly.

"It looks like Buzz's pistol," Ace said. "A Colt Model 1911 45 ACP. A standard U.S. Army pistol for nearly a hundred years. I gave Buzz and Chip each one as a twenty-first-birthday present. And each of them had initials engraved on the back strap."

"Then Chip has one like it?"

"Yes. Identical, except for the serial number and the initials."

"Where is that one?"

"I don't know if he brought it along on this trip or not. He left this morning to go back, but he was going to stop in Chicago for a couple of days."

Hogan nodded. "I'll put a hurry-up on the ballistics check, but I can't say for sure how long it will be."

"Sure."

Ace turned away from Hogan. He looked even more tired than Sissy. I wondered if either of them had had a good night's sleep since Buzz had been killed. Exhaustion is certainly a symptom of unresolved grief.

Ace came toward us. For once I didn't have the feeling that he was going to pick a fight with Sissy. Maybe he would simply leave quietly, and then Sissy and I could leave quietly, and we'd all have a quiet evening. If Ace would just not say anything.

So I was surprised when Sissy stood up. "Ace," she said, "I'm sorry."

I wouldn't have thought Ace could look more pale and drawn than he already did, but he managed it.

"I'm sorry," Sissy said again. "I've been at fault for not realizing how much Buzz's death hurt you."

She picked up an umbrella that had been resting against her chair, and she turned toward the door. She obviously didn't expect an answer from Ace.

I followed her, but Ace surprised us.

"Sissy," he said, "I owe you an apology, too. I've blamed you for Buzz's death. I'm sorry."

Then he extended his hand. Sissy eyed it warily, but in a few seconds she extended hers, and they shook. They stared into each other's eyes, communicating in some word-less way that definitely left us bystanders out.

"Friends," Ace said.

"Sure," Sissy said. "Friends."

I was dying to know what inspired this love feast, but I decided this was one time I'd keep my mouth shut. I was surprised that Sissy had one more thing to say.

"I'll let you handle this," she said, "but be careful. Be very careful."

CHAPTER 20

Ace laughed, though the sound had no humor in it. "I'm still the tough old soldier."

On that line he turned around and walked out. Sissy gave a final yelp.

"Ace!"

Ace didn't react. He simply left.

I was completely mystified. "Sissy," I said, "what was all that about?"

She didn't seem to hear me. She was staring after Ace, a worried look on her face. I repeated my question. Again, she didn't answer. Then she shook her head and seemed to come to herself.

"Sorry to hold you up," she said. "I'm ready if you are."

Joe had appeared, and the three of us headed for the door. Sissy was still brandishing the umbrella. When I asked where she had gotten it, she said that Hogan dug it out of the city's lost and found. "He swears it's been there a year," she said. "If somebody stops me on the street and demands his umbrella back, I'll give it to him."

We were nearly out the door when Hogan called Sissy's name.

"Listen, Sissy," he said. "If you think of anything you want to tell me, give me a call." He walked over and handed her a business card. "I wrote my cell number on the back of this. I'll have it on all night."

"I think Ace is the one who'll be calling," Sissy said. She went on out the door.

And we went out into sunshine. The rain was over, the sun was out, and the lost-and-found umbrella wasn't needed. Joe, Sissy, and I climbed into his truck, sitting three in a row.

As soon as we were in, I took a deep breath, ready to ask Sissy what the heck was going on between Ace and her, but before I could expel that breath through my vocal cords, Joe spoke.

"Okay, Sissy," he said. "What was it you didn't tell Hogan?"

"I told him the truth."

"I'm sure you did. But you didn't tell him the whole truth. And, Sissy, he knows you didn't."

"I answered every question, Joe. Truthfully."

"What didn't Hogan ask?"

This time Sissy didn't answer. Joe spoke again. "If it's a privileged communication, we'll throw Lee out of the truck, and you can tell me."

"No, Joe. You heard everything I had to say."

I couldn't restrain myself any longer. "What is Ace going to take care of?"

Sissy gave me an incredibly innocent look. "He's working with Hogan to identify the pistol."

I spoke again. "What in all this inspired you to make a peace gesture toward Ace?"

"He just looked so — so much like I feel, I guess. Besides, in the past, he seemed to blame me. Either he thought I shot Buzz or that I did something that caused his death. And today he didn't."

Neither Joe nor I asked any more questions. I guess I would have, but I couldn't think of any. Sissy declined something to eat, saying she'd like to get home before dark. Although it was after eight o'clock, it was mid-June, close to the longest day of the year. Our area of Michigan stays light until nearly ten in mid-June. Joe took the road east out of Warner Pier.

But even though I didn't ask any questions, I thought like crazy. Obviously, Sissy and Ace had come to some sort of under-

255

standing, and it had focused on the gun found in Sissy's Volkswagen. But Joe had been there for the whole episode, and he didn't understand it either. I wondered if Hogan did. Hogan never missed much.

We let the subject drop for the twenty minutes it took to reach Moose Lodge. When we got there, the sun was still out, but it was dropping toward the horizon, so that rich golden light that glows when it's almost sundown was coming through the trees. Wildflower was standing in the door-way of the house, carrying Johnny, who held out his arms and called, "Mama!" The place looked so welcoming, I almost wanted to go in myself. But I didn't. Joe made sure that Sissy had his phone number as well as Ho-gan's; then we headed west, toward Warner Pier.

But I was still thinking about Moose Lodge. Its rustic atmosphere had appealed to me from the first moment I saw it. On my next visit, I had parked in the yard next to Chip's rental car . . .

And at the moment I was visualizing my memories of Moose Lodge, one of those wild coincidences that life hands us struck.

A yellow car loomed up in the other lane, heading east. It came toward us and passed.

"Joe! Pull over," I said.

256

"What's wrong?"

"Nothing! I just have to think about something. It's important!"

"Lee, there's no place to pull over here." He was right. The shoulder on that stretch of road is almost nonexistent.

"The nature preserve parking lot is right down the next road. Stop there!"

"Well, okay. But you'd better have a good explanation. I'm ready for dinner."

After we were stopped in the parking lot, Joe turned sideways, leaning against the door, and stared at me. "You're obviously having one of your brain waves. What's going on in that beautiful blond head?"

"I just had a flashback to the second time I came out to Moose Lodge. Let me tell you about it, and you tell me if I'm making sense."

"Carry on."

"I parked the van around by the shop. And there was a silver or gray car, a midsized sedan, already parked in the next space over."

"So?"

"So when I went into the shop, Chip was there."

"So?"

"Joe, he was driving the car parked outside, a midsized silver sedan. But when we met him at the Willard General Store, he was driving a flashy yellow compact. Both of them had rental stickers on the bumper. Same company."

"Why would he change?"

"Maybe the ashtrays got full, and he demanded a new vehicle. I don't know. But I do know one thing that happened between the time I ran into him at Moose Lodge and our lunch at the General Store. In the meantime, somebody chased me through the nature preserve."

"You didn't see who it was."

"No. But I did see a midsized silver or gray sedan pull out of this very parking lot."

Joe frowned. "You think it was Chip? Why would he chase you?"

"Because the person who chased me had destroyed the tracks a prowler made out by the Reagans' garage, and he didn't want me to see who it was. So the real question is, why would Chip destroy those tracks?"

"Because they were incriminating for some reason."

"Right. Like maybe they were made by him."

"But why would Chip prowl around either the Reagans' place or Moose Lodge?"

"Because he's looking for some sort of papers."

"How do you know that?"

"Because the other day a prowler went through the desks used by both Wildflower and Sissy." I tapped a finger on Joe's chest for emphasis. "And the person who killed Buzz also went through the desks. Plus, he destroyed files from Buzz's computer."

"You think Chip might have done that? But Chip denied knowing anything about Buzz's novel. And he was supposedly Buzz's best friend."

"True. So, why has Sissy been the main suspect in Buzz's death?"

"Because she was Buzz's wife." Joe nodded. "I know, I know. The people closest to the victim are the most obvious suspects."

"Yes. Now the catch is that Chip was apparently abroad — working for that defense contractor in some exotic spot — when Buzz died."

"That can be checked."

"I know. But Chip already blew that story. At the Willard General Store. When I commented on how crowded the place was with its oddball stock, he said, 'You should have seen it last February, when they were painting.' Or something like that. If Chip was abroad, how did he know the General Store was painted in February?"

"You're right. He did say that. And if he

259

was somewhere abroad, he wouldn't have known."

"Plus, Joe — something about that pistol made both Ace and Sissy change their whole opinions of each other. You saw them at the police department! It was a regular love feast! And every other time they've been together, it was a dogfight. That pistol was key to the whole change in their attitudes."

I leaned toward him. "Rosy Reagan teased Wildflower because she doesn't want firearms on the Moose Lodge property. What do you bet that when Buzz moved in there, he took his pistol — the special one his dad had given him — to Ace's house and left it there? He wouldn't want to get rid of it, but he would have wanted to respect Wildflower's wishes, too."

I took a deep breath. "So, if he was shot with that pistol, the shooter had to have access to Ace's house! And Sissy and Ace knew it."

"Chip again!"

"Right. And Helen."

"Right! Helen could have figured out that the pistol had been used."

"She could also have figured out that the house had been used. If Ace was in Florida when Chip showed up to try to get his important papers from Buzz, why would he go to a hotel? Ace's house is a year-round house. Chip could simply have stayed there. Even if he tried to hide that he had slept or eaten there — there are dozens of ways Helen could have figured it out."

"McDonald's sacks in the trash."

"Sure. Or used towels. For someone familiar with the household routine, it would have been a snap. She lived on the property. If someone had been staying at Ace's house, she would have known."

I pulled out my cell phone. "You're not poking any holes in this, Joe."

"That's because I'm afraid you're right."

I called information.

"Who are you calling?"

"Sissy."

"Why her? Why now?"

"Because of the yellow compact."

"What yellow compact?"

"The car that passed us, going east, just before I yelled for you to pull in here."

"I didn't see it."

"You were looking into the sun. I couldn't see it clearly either until it was past us. Then I looked back, and I saw it. I'm afraid it was Chip."

"But Ace said Chip left to go back to — to this exotic place where he's working, wherever it is."

"Let's just make sure."

I called information and got the number for a person named Hill, east of Warner Pier, then punched the magic button that automatically called Sissy and Wildflower. After five rings I got an answering machine. I didn't leave a message.

Joe frowned. "I can't believe Sissy wouldn't pick up, Lee. After all, you're her boss."

"Joe, Wildflower doesn't have caller ID. She told me."

"But they can't have gone anywhere. Sissy wanted to put Johnny to bed. I suppose they might have gone out to the shop."

"Wildflower has a phone extension in the shop. It was sitting on a display case right beside a cute little black squirrel."

Joe started the truck. "We'd better go back and check."

CHAPTER 21

"Now wait a minute!" I said. "Let's not rush into this."

"What do you mean?"

"I mean stop the truck a minute, and let's talk tactics."

Joe halted the truck just before its nose reached the road. He kept the motor running, but he turned toward me with a questioning look.

"Okay," I said. "Let's plan for the worst-case scenario. Let's assume Chip really is over at Moose Lodge. We can't just bull into the place. He'll shoot somebody."

"I thought I could walk quietly down Wildflower's drive and peek through the bushes. I should be able to see if that yellow car is parked by the house."

"What if it's parked behind the house?"

He frowned. "I see what you mean. I might need to go to the door and ask if everything's okay."

"And if it's not, Chip might —" I stopped. I didn't want to think about what Chip might do.

Joe and I both stared into space for a moment. "Maybe we'd better consult Hogan," he said. "I didn't want to call him if it was nothing, but if it's something . . ."

I held up my cell phone.

"I'll use mine." Joe punched the button that called Hogan's cell phone. "Busy," he said. "I'll try the office." All he got from the dispatcher was a promise to give Hogan a message.

"I'll call the house," I said. "Maybe Hogan actually went home to dinner."

But that line was busy, too. "Darn!" I said. "Hogan and Aunt Nettie are probably talking to each other."

"We can't wait," Joe said. He put the truck in gear and headed toward Moose Lodge. "Now, here's the plan. You get out of the truck there by the old fruit stand. You keep trying to call Hogan. I go on down the drive, just as if this were a casual call. Do you have a notebook or some sort of papers?"

"No. I left all that in my van."

"Then reach around behind my seat. I've got some papers back there. It's a receipt for varnish, but it'll look official."

I got the papers and found a marking pen in my purse. I used it to write, "Is everything okay?" in big letters across the varnish receipt.

"Good," Joe said. "If I can get that to Sissy or Wildflower, they ought to get the picture."

"Joe, Sissy works for me, not you. Wouldn't it be more logical for me to be the one who goes down to the house with papers for Sissy?"

"Lee, do you have a gun?"

"No. I don't routinely carry a gun. And neither do you."

"How about Chip?"

"I'm afraid he's likely to have a gun. But I don't want to shoot anybody! I just want to figure out if they need help. I don't even want to hit anybody."

"I don't want to hit anybody either. But if it becomes necessary, Lee, frankly, I think I'm better at hitting people than you are."

"You were a high school wrestling champ. Chip is probably trained in combat techniques. That's a whole different thing."

"Even so, I can hit harder than you can."

"Nah! Nah! But you're not bulletproof!"

"In this case, Lee, I am. I've got to be."

Joe swung the truck into the drive of Moose Lodge and stopped. "Out. And be sure you have your phone."

"Joe! I don't want you to go alone!"

I'd always wondered exactly what the word "hauteur" meant. Now I knew. It meant the look I got from Joe at that moment. And that particular look at that particular time could have been translated as "A man's gotta do what a man's gotta do." It might be logical for me, rather than for Joe, to approach Moose Lodge, but he wasn't going to let his woman go into danger.

"Out," Joe said. His voice was as firm as I'd ever heard it.

I got out of the truck. There are times when even a liberated, modern woman has to respect her man's pride.

"I'll keep calling Hogan," I said. "And be careful!"

"The whole thing is probably all in our imaginations."

I got out, closing the door gently so that it wouldn't make a noise in the quiet country atmosphere. Then Joe drove off.

Darn him! Joe wasn't bulletproof. But he was strong, and he really had once been a state wrestling champ. Joe doesn't pick fights, but a couple of times one had picked him, and when he grabbed his opponent, the opponent stayed grabbed. I had to respect his wishes.

I pushed the knowledge that Chip was probably trained in hand-to-hand fighting down into my subconscious.

Over and over, I muttered a phrase as I punched Hogan's cell phone number. "Joe is bulletproof. Joe is bulletproof."

I was so relieved when Hogan answered his phone that I said it out loud.

"Joe is bulletproof! Hogan! You're there!"

"Yes, Lee. I just got home. And I'm glad to hear that Joe has unusual powers. But what are you talking about?"

It took me a couple of minutes to explain. First, I had to tell Hogan why Joe and I thought Chip was at Moose Lodge. Second, I had to clarify why we considered him a likely menace, and third, explain that Joe had gone down to the house to see what was going on.

Even without a cell phone I probably could have heard Hogan's roar across the fifteen miles from Moose Lodge to Warner Pier.

"You two are going to be the death of yourselves and me, too! Where are you now?"

"I'm out by the old fruit stand at Moose Lodge."

"I'll have the state police there ASAP. Don't hang up! And don't go anywhere!

Especially not down to the house."

Hogan left the phone for a minute or less. I could hear him talking in another direction. He finished up with "And no sirens!"

Then he was back on the phone. "Well, as long as you're there, tiptoe down to the turn in the drive and peek through the bushes. Tell me if you can see anything. For God's sake, don't let anybody see you from the house!"

Clinging to my phone and shaking in every limb, I obeyed his command.

The buildings on the Moose Lodge property were beautiful as the setting sun dappled through the trees. Joe's truck was sitting in front of the larger house. There was no sign of the yellow rental car.

"But something's happening," I told Hogan in a whisper. "Joe wouldn't have left me this long to stand here and be afraid of what was happening to him. I mean, I'll murder him if he just left me hanging here when there's nothing wrong. But, Hogan, Joe and I have just been guessing about Chip. We could be wrong."

"You're not wrong," he said grimly. "Ace checked. He was able to get hold of Chip's boss — wherever the hell Chip's assigned by that mysterious company that supposedly is working for the United States in some obscure corner of the world. Chip was on leave when Buzz was killed. So he lied about that. And Buzz had left his gun in a closet at Ace's house. Chip had access to it."

"Oh! But maybe that wasn't the gun that killed Buzz."

"How likely do you think that is?"

When I spoke again, I could tell how small my voice was. "I was hoping I was wrong."

"Lee, stay on the phone. Go back to the fruit stand and stay there. Keep out of sight of the house. I'm in my car and on the way. Don't hang up until I get there. Or until the state police get there. One of us will be there momentarily."

But the first car to arrive was not official. It was a large black Buick, and the first person to get out was Colonel Ace Smith. He ran over to me.

"Where is he?"

I wasn't sure if he meant Chip or Joe. But the answer was the same. "I think he's down at the main house."

"He needs to walk out on his own."

I decided he meant Chip. "Hogan will give him a chance to do that. The last thing they want is some kind of gun battle."

"No, no!" Ace put his hand up to his head, and I thought he was going to tear out a handful of hair. Then he took a few steps down the road, toward the house.

Before he could get to the first bank of trees, Hogan's patrol car pulled in, followed closely by a Michigan State Police car. Ace turned around and came back to meet them. The lawmen parked silently, with no throwing up of gravel or squealing of brakes. Both men jumped out of their vehicles. No one spoke to me, but the lawmen and Ace gathered in a clump and conferred. There was a lot of arm waving, fist punching, and excited whispering.

Then Ace spoke. "I'm going down there." He moved toward the drive again. Hogan and the state police officer got even more excited, and the state policeman blocked Ace's path.

The whole episode looked ridiculous because they were all determined not to make any noise. There was whispering, gesturing, foot stomping — the whole works — but not a sound. It was ridiculous — but not funny.

Finally, Hogan was apparently able to lay down the law to Ace. Ace wasn't to go in on his own — absolutely not.

Ace came and stood beside me, staring at the ground. I felt a lot of sympathy for him. I wanted to be in there, too. I was willing to recognize that I might cause more problems, but I wanted to be in there. Not knowing what was going on was torturing me.

I spoke to Ace quietly. "I'm sorry, Colonel Smith."

"He's ruined. Maybe it's best if he dies."

"No! No one should get hurt."

Ace and I exchanged a long look. "Chip's got to be given a chance to walk out, to surrender quietly. And I've got to know why."

"Why?"

"Why Chip went haywire like this." His eyes narrowed. "Your husband's in there, right?"

I nodded.

Ace moved his mouth close to my ear. "Is there a back way in?"

"Just from the nature preserve. Oh! And there's a path from the neighbor's house."

"Is it screened from the Moose Lodge house?"

"In there everything's screened from everything else. There's an unbelievable number of trees."

He squeezed my arm. "Let's go."

Right then I should have turned my back on him and walked away.

But I didn't. I pulled my arm out of his grasp, and I slowly began to walk toward the gravel road where all the law-enforcement cars were parked.

Hogan saw me and spoke, still keeping his voice quiet. "Where are you going?"

And I told a lie. "I'm going over to the Reagans' house," I said. "If they see all these cars, they'll be running over to tell Wildflower something's going on."

"Good idea," Hogan said.

CHAPTER 22

Hogan didn't ask why Ace was going to the Reagans' with me. This, I think, was because of dumb luck. Two more state police cars and the other Warner Pier patrolman arrived just at that time, and they distracted Hogan.

Ace and I ignored the newcomers and walked briskly down the road toward the Reagans' place. We didn't run until we got to their drive.

I was glad to see that Nosy and Rosy's truck wasn't parked in their drive. Nosy was bound to want to get his pistol, and the whole thing would go better, or I thought it would, if we didn't have an amateur gunman mixing in. And I couldn't imagine Rosy not getting out his gun if he knew there was a hostage standoff next door.

If there was going to be a hostage standoff. After all, we didn't know for sure.

I led Ace around the double-wide and

back to the garage and workshop. It was still easy to find the path, even though the light was beginning to fail. Nosy and Rosy's property was even more thickly wooded than Moose Lodge, and things were getting murky as the sun kept on going down.

"I wish I'd thought to get a flashlight from the truck," I said.

Ace promptly pulled a flashlight from the pocket of his Windbreaker.

"You're a regular Boy Scout," I said.

I led the way. For once I was glad that TenHuis Chocolade encouraged its sales and business office employees to wear chocolate brown shirts, khakis, and tennis shoes. At least I wasn't trotting down a forest path in high heels, and I was wearing inconspicuous colors.

We passed the junk pile and kept on. "Aren't we headed in the wrong direction?" Ace said.

"We'll hit a fork soon."

We came to the fence that marked the Moose Lodge property line. When we reached the fork in the path and swung back toward the south, Ace gave a grunt of satisfaction.

"Slow down now," I whispered. "We're close to the house."

The big metal shop building loomed up

in the twilight. Ace and I crept to its corner and peeked around it. The yellow rental car was sitting in the gravel parking lot in front of the shop.

I wasn't happy to see it. I guess I'd still had some hope that Joe and I had imagined the whole situation.

The shop's windows were dark. The smaller house — the one where Sissy and Buzz had lived — was off to the right. Joe's truck was parked beside it. That house also looked completely deserted, its windows dark.

But light poured from Wildflower's house. Obviously every light was on in the central room — the combined kitchen, dining room, and living room — and just as obviously no window had a shade or curtain. And there were windows on three sides of the big room, so it was illuminating quite a bit of the outside.

How were we going to get a look in that big room? If we looked in those windows, the people inside could easily see us.

I took a step toward the main building, but Ace grabbed my arm. He whispered in my ear. "Go back now."

I stared at him in disbelief. I shook my head.

"Yes," he said. "Go back!"

275

"No!" I mouthed the word.

"You don't even have a weapon." He pulled out a pistol.

I gave him what I hoped was a scathing look and whispered again. "If you shoot the wrong person, I won't need a weapon. I'll kill you with my bare hands."

I shook his hand off my arm and ran forward on tiptoes. I managed to skirt the gravel parking area and to avoid snapping any twigs, so I was able to move quietly. I got to the house and stood with my back to the wall. Then I sidled along until I was beside one of the windows. Thanks to the mild evening and Wildflower's belief in fresh air, the window was cracked open.

Peeking in at the corner, I saw that there was a high-backed chair in front of the window, an old-fashioned rocking chair with a heavy board at the top. Good, it would shield me from whoever was inside the window.

I heard Chip's voice; it sounded as if he were right beside me. And I realized he was. He was sitting in the chair. By some enormous piece of luck, I'd come up behind him.

"Let's go over it one more time," he said. "Buzz told me you have secret hiding places at Moose Lodge. And he used one of them to hide something I sent him. Now I've got to find it. If you help me, I'll be out of here in a flash."

Sissy spoke. "Chip, I think Buzz would have told me if he hid something. I mean, I might have stumbled over it and thrown it out or something. I don't believe he did that."

"I believe he did, Sissy."

"We could look, I suppose." This was Wildflower's voice. "The only place I can think of is the rock in the fireplace. I haven't looked in there in years."

"Well, let's look now." Chip's voice wasn't friendly.

The rocking chair moved vigorously, and I ducked. Chip had stood up. I could see part of the room. Sissy was sitting in the other rocking chair — the twiggy one. She was rocking Johnny, and he seemed to be asleep. Wildflower and Chip were kneeling by the fireplace. Wildflower pulled a stone from the hearth. Chip eagerly looked in the hole it uncovered.

Then he swore. "Not there! But that place wouldn't hide a stash from the cops."

"What makes you think we ever wanted to do that?"

"Oh, come on, Ms. Hippie! Where else can we look?"

"I suppose you've looked places like the backs of the commodes or in the sugar canister."

"Do you think I'm an idiot? Of course I looked in the obvious places. This is one of your hippie-dippie trickie deals! Where! Where!"

Sissy spoke sharply. "Quit yelling at my grandmother, Chip! If you were so eager to find this mysterious object, you shouldn't have shot Buzz!"

"Believe me — I didn't mean to!"

That exchange chilled me clean down to every bone I owned. Chip had tried to make it sound as if he wanted cooperation in finding the object Buzz had hidden. But now he had admitted to killing Buzz.

But Chip was still talking. "I didn't want to hurt anybody! Especially not Buzz! But the jerk never went anywhere. He just stayed around here. So did your grandmother. I couldn't get onto the property to look for my stuff. Finally — finally — I thought I saw you and your grandmother leave, and then the other car left. I thought the place was deserted."

Chip sounded disheartened. He was being much too frank. I feared that meant he would have to kill Wildflower and Sissy.

That scared me. But it didn't scare me as

much as something else did.

Where was Joe?

And where was Ace?

I ducked down and looked around. No one was in sight.

Just me. Actually, I wasn't worried about Ace. First, we had no emotional connection. Second, he had a pistol, and he could take care of himself.

Joe can take care of himself, too — usually. But I doubted his claim to be bulletproof. Where could he be? It was useless to look for him. He didn't seem to be in the room with Wildflower, Sissy, and Chip, but there were a million bushes and trees on the Moose Lodge property, and Joe could be under or behind any of them.

Actually, I didn't expect him to be under or behind anything. He was much more likely to be in the thick of things.

But regardless of where Joe was, I knew where I was. I was on my own. I could find my way back to the path over to Nosy and Rosy's house — there was just about enough light left for me to get there. That was the sensible thing to do. It was the thing both Joe and Hogan would want me to do.

But I just couldn't do it. I'm always convinced no one can manage unless I stick my nose into any situation.

I peeked in the window again, and I heard Sissy. "Look — Johnny's getting heavy. He's sound asleep. Let me take him into his room and put him in his crib. Then I can help look."

Chip looked unconvinced, and Sissy spoke again. "I know you don't want to hurt Johnny, Chip. Let me put him in a safe place."

"Okay. But we all three stick together."

"Fine." Sissy's voice was calm and controlled.

Aha! So they were going into the bedroom end of the house. All three — Chip, Sissy, and Wildflower.

That meant the kitchen end would be deserted, including that mudroom near the back door. I could slip in and hide in there.

If I wanted to. Did I? I could hear everything from there, and I could see a lot, but no one could see me.

It would sure put me in a good position for joining the party. It might also put me in a good position for getting killed.

But hanging around outside didn't put me in any position at all. I might be able to tell Hogan what happened after I'd witnessed it, but I sure wasn't going to influence matters.

All this analysis takes longer to describe

than it took for it to race through my head. Sissy, Wildflower, and Chip had barely disappeared into the bedroom hall when I was at the back door.

As I expected, given what Wildflower had said about her door-locking habits, the door was not locked. I eased it open, trying not to even allow the lock to click. And I was in the mudroom. It was dark. Feeling carefully to make sure I didn't kick a minnow bucket or knock down a snow shovel, I edged into the room — actually nothing but a big closet.

I stood there silently, and I began to be aware of my surroundings.

Breathing. I could hear breathing. Coffee. I could smell coffee breath.

I wasn't alone. Someone else was in the closet with me.

Before I could fling the door open and leap out, a strong arm flung around my shoulders, and a strong hand clamped over my mouth.

CHAPTER 23

It's hard to yell in a whisper, but the person holding me managed. "Lee! Lee!"

I had found Joe.

"Lee? Can I let you go?"

I nodded. And Joe slowly loosened his grip.

I whispered. "Yeech, Joe. I won't need a heart checkup this year."

He whispered back. "I couldn't take a chance on your bumping into me in the dark. I'm sorry if I startled you."

"Startled is not a strong enough word. What are you doing in here?"

"Trying to figure out what's going on and see if I can get the jump on Chip. What are you doing here?"

"Same thing you are, only I hadn't thought as far as attacking Chip. Hogan's gathering his forces at the road. They ought to be here with a bullhorn any minute."

"Great. Then we'll have to come out with

our hands up or get shot."

"Ace is wandering around with a pistol, too."

"Super." Only Joe can sound sarcastic in a whisper.

"Maybe we should sneak out the back way and take the path over to the Reagans'."

"Maybe you should. But I can't leave Wildflower and Sissy here."

"Mr. Chivalry."

"Do you want me to leave them?"

"I guess not. But it might be smarter to let Hogan handle the situation under proper hostage negotiation rules."

"You can slip out the back and tell Hogan what the situation is."

"I'm not leaving you."

We hadn't raised our voices, but we sure had reached an impasse. But that never lasts long with Joe. He's the original man of action — and ideas.

"Okay," he said. "As long as you're here. You sneak out the back. When you're outside, I'll crawl into the kitchen and hide behind the counter. You go around the house and pound on the front door. Chip looks at you, and I grab him from behind."

"An alternative plan is that we stay here until Hogan and the gang arrive."

At that moment Wildflower came back

down the bedroom hall, followed closely by Sissy and Chip.

Everything still looked calm, but there was one change. Chip was holding a pistol.

"Okay!" he said. "Now Johnny's settled, so you can concentrate on my problem. Where did Buzz hide the papers? I've got to know, and I've got to know now!"

He grabbed Wildflower and pushed her over in front of the fireplace. Then he raised the pistol and pointed it at her. "Sissy! You don't have to worry about Johnny. So you'd better worry about your grandmother."

"No!" Sissy sounded stricken. "Chip, she doesn't know or care about some old letters you wrote."

Chip stared at her, but he kept the gun pointed at Wildflower.

Joe whispered. "That rips it. Chip hadn't said they were letters."

"Oh," Chip said, "so you do know about them."

"I *don't* know!"

"Buzz told you."

"No, Chip. He didn't tell me anything. But the only contact the two of you had was by mail. You used to gripe about it. If Buzz had your papers, it had to be letters."

"Don't tell him anything," Wildflower said calmly. "If Chip finds whatever he's looking for, he'll kill us both."

"No!" Chip yelled the word. "I don't want to hurt anybody. I just want my papers! Okay, my letters."

"We can't wait," Joe said. "Slip out and go around to the front door." He grabbed my arm. "Then duck away from the door. There's always the chance he'll shoot at it. God, I hate this, but we've got to do something!"

I didn't have any alternate plan, but I sure hated for Joe to attack a guy younger than he was and trained in hand-to-hand combat. I took a deep breath and got ready to go out that back door.

But Joe's desperate whisper may have been a prayer, because a miracle happened.

The British play a kind of hide-and-seek they call "sardines." When they find the player who's "it," each seeker joins him in his hiding place. This leads to a half dozen or so people crammed into one hiding place.

Joe's plea seemed to have kicked off a game of sardines.

The back door opened, and Ace walked in. He ignored Joe and me. He simply stood there, not two feet from us, and looked through the kitchen and into the living room for at least a minute.

Looking back, I'm sure he had no idea we

were even there. And Joe and I were so surprised that we both stood absolutely still. In a mad way, I wanted to laugh. It was like a theatrical farce.

It was just darn lucky Ace didn't turn around, because he probably would have been so surprised to see us that he would have shot us both.

Chip was still yelling at Sissy. "Tell me! Tell me! I've got to have those papers!"

Sissy yelled back. "We don't have them!"

"I know there are hiding places in this house!"

"That's crazy!"

"Tell me!" Chip stepped close to Wild-flower and aimed the pistol at her head. "Tell me!"

That was when Ace moved.

"Chip!" He snapped out the word. Then he strode through the kitchen in three or four paces and went on into the living room. He was holding his own pistol, but it was down by his side.

"Chip, put that pistol down," he said. "Stop acting like an idiot!"

Chip whirled to meet him. "Ace! Where did you come from?"

"I came in the back door. You didn't even secure your perimeter. Plus, every state cop in Michigan is out there at the road, and they'll be down here to take you out any minute."

"State cops!"

"Yes. State cops. So put the pistol down and go quietly."

"But, Ace, I did all this to protect you!"

"Did I need your help?"

"Oh, I admit it was my fault. I sent a copy of that stupid report to Buzz. It never occurred to me that he'd use it in his novel!"

"You should never have sent it in the first place."

"Ace, it was horrible over there. Buzz couldn't take it and came home. I was the one who toughed it out. But I needed someone to talk to; it was the only thing that helped."

"Talk is one thing. Stealing that report is another."

"I just wanted Buzz to see what we were up against. And I was trying to get it back!"

"You didn't have to kill my son to get it."

"He was a traitor to you, Ace!"

"Maybe I was a traitor to him. Put the gun down."

"I thought I was doing the right thing! What you wanted me to do!"

"Put the gun down."

"No! I'll use it!" Chip raised his pistol and pointed it at Ace. "Should I use it on you?"

He swung the gun around toward himself. "Or on me?"

"Put it down!" Ace roared the command.

Chip hesitated, still pointing the gun toward himself.

Behind him, Wildflower gave a disgusted grunt. "Oh, for heaven's sake!" she said. "Cut the cackle!"

Chip kept looking at Ace. He couldn't see her as, in one smooth motion, she grabbed the fireplace poker, swung it, and hit him in the back of the head.

Chip fell, but only to his knees; then he dropped his pistol.

Joe and I ran forward, but Ace didn't move.

He simply stood and watched as I scooped up Chip's pistol, and Joe clamped a hammerlock on the stunned man.

Ace lowered his gun to his side, then continued to stand there stoically as I pulled out my cell phone and called Hogan.

"Well, Gran," Sissy said, "you sure picked the right time to forget about nonviolence."

The next hour was wild, of course. All kinds of law officers poured in. Even Burt Ramsey was there. He ate crow over Chip's confession — with four witnesses — to killing Buzz, then Helen Ferguson. He wasn't very gracious about it.

After Chip had been taken away, Hogan spoke firmly to Sissy and Ace. "We could have avoided all this excitement if you two had told me Chip was guilty this afternoon, when you realized where Buzz's gun came from."

"But I wasn't sure," Sissy said. "I knew Buzz had taken his pistol back to Ace's house, because Gran didn't want firearms at Moose Lodge. But after Buzz was killed, nobody ever asked us about it. The investigators just asked if there were any guns on the premises. The fact that Buzz used to have a gun didn't cross my mind, much less that it had been used to kill him. Then this afternoon, it fell out of my glove compartment. Of course, I remembered it had been at Ace's house, which meant that Chip was the logical person to have access to it."

"I had access to it, too," Ace said.

"I never suspected you, Ace," Sissy said. "I was awfully angry with you — in some ways I still am — but I never doubted that you loved Buzz. In your own way. No, the other person I suspected was Helen Ferguson."

Ace gave a wry smile. "The boys tried to tell me she snooped, but it was so handy having her as a cleaning woman that I ignored it."

He turned to Hogan. "I'm willing to bet that she told Chip she knew the gun was there."

"Colonel Smith," I said, "did you once own a blue Volkswagen, an older one?"

"I still own it," he said. "It's in the big storage shed."

"Oh," I said. "I think Helen told Chip she knew he'd used that car to drive over here the day he killed Buzz. I think she had been blackmailing him."

Nobody denied that.

Ace looked sadder than I'd ever seen anyone look. "Whatever happened with Helen," he said, "Chip could have broken her neck on the spot. He was an expert in hand-to-hand combat."

"It may not have been premeditated," Sissy said.

But Ace shook his head. "Killing her might not have been premeditated. But he used Helen's phone to text you. He made a deliberate attempt to frame you. That was unforgivable."

Sissy shuddered. "I'll never forgive him for standing out on the beach, in the dark, and watching me as I found her body. I saw him against the reflection on the water. He nearly scared me to death."

Hogan nodded. "We'll never know exactly

what happened unless Chip decides to tell us. But why didn't you and Sissy share this knowledge about Chip this afternoon?"

Sissy sighed. "Mainly I couldn't believe it. Chip and Buzz were such close friends. And I was still thinking that Chip had been abroad when Buzz died. And when I began to doubt that — well, I trusted Ace to check it out."

"Yes," Ace said. "And I called you, Hogan, as soon as I talked to Chip's boss. But the fact that Chip was on leave when Buzz died didn't prove he'd flown halfway around the world to kill his best friend."

Hogan left then, and after a few more minutes, Joe and I got up to leave. "Sissy," I said, "take tomorrow off. TenHuis won't go under if you and I sleep all day."

"You can tell you don't have a fourteen-month-old," Sissy said. "Sleeping all day is not an option for me."

After we'd all laughed, Wildflower spoke. "Actually, I'm hoping you and Joe will come back for dinner tomorrow. And Ace, I'd like you to come, too."

We must have looked puzzled, because she went on. "There are a few things all of you should know."

How could we resist an invitation like that?

CHAPTER 24

The next day we all showed up at Moose Lodge around six o'clock. Johnny was in his high chair, wearing footie pajamas and a large bib. Sissy was poking his dinner into his mouth. He'd eat a bite of beets, then pick up a few Cheerios from his tray.

Ace came in just after us. He went over to speak to his grandson, talking to him quite as if the baby were an adult. When Johnny sprayed a combination of beets and spit on him, Ace just laughed.

"Sissy, I hope you'll let me see Johnny now and then," he said. No one mentioned the custody suit.

"I'm sure we can work something out." Sissy shook a finger at him. "But don't plan on military school. I still hold to my grandmother's nonviolent principles."

Ace looked at Wildflower and made a swinging motion, a lot like the one she'd used to fell Chip. "Your grandmother knows how to ignore theory when she needs to get practical results," he said. "A mighty tough lady. And I mean that as a compliment."

Wildflower looked a bit flustered. She handed Ace a wet washcloth, which he used to get the beets off his face. Then she served all of us a glass of Michigan wine. We sat in her comfortable living room on her rustic furniture. The evening was cool enough for a small fire in the fireplace.

As soon as his dinner was over, Johnny was placed in the middle of the floor and given a set of blocks to play with. Of course, he found all these new people much more interesting than blocks, so he cruised around, looking each of us over, holding on to our knees, and giving each of us a big friendly smile.

I didn't know if I should make polite conversation or leave it to our hostess. I didn't have to wait long.

Ace turned to Sissy. "I know Buzz didn't leave you anything, Sissy. He hadn't even worked enough quarters to leave Social Security benefits. I wish I could say I'll make up the deficit, but I'm going to have to admit something that embarrasses me. As you probably all know, I inherited quite a bit of money from my mother. But my legal bills over the Dobermann-Smith scandal have wiped me out. That's why I sold the Chicago house and moved to Warner Pier. I'll try to help with Johnny's upbringing and education, but my main income is my military retirement. And I'm in debt, including a big mortgage on the lakeshore house. I can help you a little, month to month, but there won't be much when I'm gone."

"Oh, Ace," Sissy said. "I don't expect help! Gran raised me to stand on my own." She grinned. "And now she tells me I'm going to Michigan State, whether I want to or not."

"Oh, Sissy!" Wildflower shook her head. Then she spoke to all of us. "It wasn't until we were in the middle of all this mess that I understood I'd misled the whole community, and even my own family, by the way I live. When I discovered that Sissy had consulted a poverty law firm — well, I was so embarrassed, I didn't know what to do."

She turned to Joe. "Your agency does wonderful work. I've supported it for years."

Joe gaped slightly. "You have?"

"Right. Through the Fox Foundation."

"You're part of the Fox Foundation?"

"I'm afraid so. Before I married Andrew Hill and changed my name to Wildflower Hill, I was Celestia Fox."

This brought laughter from Joe and an amazed gasp from me. "Oh my gosh!" I said. "We've wondered and wondered who the Fox heiress was. The gossip is that she lives abroad."

"If you know anything about the history of the Fox family," Wildflower said, "then you know why I turned my back on money as a life value way back in my youth. I've just always preferred to live simply. By filtering my affairs through the foundation, I've managed to avoid begging letters and social obligations. I'd appreciate it if you would all help me continue to keep it quiet."

"Sure," Joe said. "But I might blackmail you to keep helping the foundation. You're our biggest private supporter."

"As long as you keep to your present policies, the foundation will support you," Wildflower said. She reached over and patted Sissy's shoulder. "And Sissy's right. I wanted her to become an independent person, not one who was always worried about money, about who wants a cut, about trying to buy happiness."

Sissy spoke sardonically. "So she didn't tell me we were filthy rich."

"I hope we're responsibly rich!" Wildflower said. "But I had never realized that the reason Sissy wouldn't let me send her away to college, for example, was that she thought I couldn't afford it. I shouldn't have misled her."

She shook a finger at her granddaughter. "But now that she knows, she'd better not go wild financially, or I'll cut her allowance to the bone."

Sissy grinned. "No designer jeans for me. Levi's are good enough."

Wildflower took a deep breath and turned to Ace. "I guess I'd better finish my speech. Chip was convinced Sissy and I were lying about the hiding places around here. Of course, he was right. When I lived out here with a group of friends, forty-plus years ago, there were things we wanted to hide . . . well, from strangers."

For "strangers," read "the law." None of us said that out loud. We all stared at Wildflower innocently.

"I left that way of life long ago. We don't have any reason to use these hidey-holes these days. But Sissy and I had shown some of them to Buzz, and there was one particular place he thought was funny. We've never looked in it since he died, but we both think it's the most likely place he would have hidden something."

She gestured. "Sissy, you do the honors."

Sissy stood up from her rustic twig rocking chair and went over to the massive hearth.

Then she walked up the chimney.

That sounds ridiculous, but that's what she did. The stones of the wide fireplace and its broad chimney were placed at different depths. A person who knew which stone to step on could walk right up it. It was a little like a climbing wall, or maybe like vertical stepping-stones.

So as we all gasped — and Joe jumped to his feet, afraid Sissy was going to fall — she climbed up the face of the fireplace until she could easily reach the huge moose head that hung near the ceiling.

Sissy pulled on its jaw, and the darn thing opened just like a trapdoor. She took out a metal box, maybe eight inches long and four inches tall.

She handed it down to Joe, then backed down the rocks. Once she was on the floor, she took the box again.

"Okay," she said. "Who gets to open it? It may be empty."

"You're Buzz's heir," Joe said. "You could open it. And your grandmother owns the house, so she certainly has the right to look at anything stored in it."

"Open it, Sissy." Wildflower's voice was firm.

297

I leaned forward eagerly, but I couldn't help noticing that Ace looked grim.

Sissy sat down in her twiggy rocker and opened the box. She reached into it and pulled out a thumb drive. "I'm willing to bet this is the backup copy of Buzz's novel," she said. "I'll keep it safe."

None of us argued with her. She put the thumb drive in her pocket, then pulled out a packet of letters held together by a rubber band. She thumbed through the return addresses. "All from Chip," she said.

"May I see?" Wildflower was at her most dignified. Sissy handed the letters over.

Wildflower looked through them. "Yes," she said, "all from Chip."

She stood up and took two steps to the fireplace. She moved the fire screen aside, leaned over, and placed the letters in the flames.

Ace jumped to his feet. "No! No! Wildflower! You can't destroy those. They may contain evidence."

"Evidence of what?"

"I'm afraid they contain embarrassing information about me."

"Pish-tosh," Wildflower said. "Joe just said I'm responsible for anything found in my house. And I can burn old letters whenever I want to."

She brushed her hands together in that traditional gesture that shows a job has been completed. "Come on, everyone. Let's eat dinner."

I wouldn't say we had a festive meal. We were all too aware that Ace had lost not one, but two sons. One of the things he told us was that Hogan had searched Chip's belongings that day, and he'd found a pair of tennis shoes with a pattern on the sole similar to the one I'd sketched. And in the clothes dryer, he found pants and a shirt in a hunter's camouflage print. These were just two more links in the chain of evidence against Chip.

But Ace told us he was hiring a lawyer for Chip — "With my legal bills, I'll barely notice the increase" — and the attorney was confident that Chip, with four witnesses to his admission that he'd killed Buzz, would avoid a trial by accepting some sort of plea bargain. It wasn't a good solution, for Chip or for Sissy either. But probably it was the one that would avoid further scandal and heartbreak.

"Chip was always troubled," Ace said. "I sent him to school after his parents split. His mother had a drinking problem, and his father just gave up and deserted the two of them. Chip was too aggressive, and Buzz was too passive, at least to my way of thinking. I thought they might even each other out. I was wrong."

He turned to Sissy. "Please try to get Buzz's novel published. I know it's going to describe a lot of stuff I'd rather people didn't know about. But it's Buzz's take on what happened. It shouldn't be suppressed."

Sissy said she now planned to enroll as a business major at Michigan State. "Someone in the English department may be able to help me decide what to do with Buzz's book," she said. "I won't rush into anything."

Toward the end of the meal, Ace called for attention. "Now," he said, "we have a serious matter to discuss. It's about my grandson. He doesn't have a nickname yet. Every boy in the Smith family has to have a nickname."

"Why is that?" Joe said.

"Because our name is Smith! A Smith has to have an unusual first name if he's going to stand out. Now, John is a perfectly fine name, but this boy is obviously going to be an outstanding person. He needs an outstanding name."

"His middle name," Sissy said, "is Fox."

"Well, that's okay," Ace said. "I guess we could call him Foxy."

"Actually," Sissy said, "Buzz had a nickname for him."

"What was it?"

"Well, Johnny was born on Friday the thirteenth, you know."

"Not Jason!" I was appalled. Joe and Sissy laughed, but Ace and Wildflower looked puzzled. Sissy explained to them that Jason was a character in a series of horror movies with *Friday the 13th* in their titles.

"No, not Jason," she said. "Buzz called him Lucky."

We all agreed it was a great nickname. "We'll call him Lucky John until he gets used to it," Wildflower said. "Then plain old Lucky."

"It's the perfect nickname," I said. "He's definitely a lucky kid. Of course, I'm not so lucky. If Sissy goes to Michigan State, I have to hire another bookkeeper."

Our grown son was home for the holidays, and, in an after-dinner discussion, he mentioned that chocolate caused him to get sores on his tongue. Then he reached for a piece of Gran's Fudge, a particularly creamy and luscious candy we make at Christmas.

"Hey!" Mom cried.

But our son shrugged. "It's already sore," he said.

Well, he's an adult. If he's willing to suffer so he can eat fudge once a year, that's his choice.

But many people have problems with chocolate. It can cause heartburn or migraines or worsen arthritis. Some people are out-and-out allergic to it, just as they may be allergic to any substance.

I'm sorry about that.

For everyone else, here's the recipe:

GRAN'S FUDGE

4 1/2 c. sugar
1 large can (10–12 oz) evaporated milk
1 jar (7 oz) marshmallow cream
18 oz semi-sweet chocolate chips
2 tbs margarine
1 tsp vanilla
Dash salt
2 c. chopped pecans

Mix sugar and milk. Cook at medium heat, stirring frequently, until the mixture reaches soft-ball stage, about ten minutes. Add marshmallow cream, chocolate chips, margarine, vanilla, salt, and pecans. Mix until smooth. Pour into nine-by-thirteen-inch buttered dish. Let set twenty-four hours.

Note: Everyone in my family uses a pressure cooker pan to make this. No, we don't use pressure. We just use the pan because it's heavy and suitable for extra-hot ingredients that shouldn't be burned or scorched. I'm lucky enough to have fallen heir to the actual pressure cooker my grandmother used, and I prize it as a special link to my family heritage.